MORTALITY BITES

MORTALITY BITES SERIES

RAMY VANCE

KEEP EVOLVING STUDIOS

To Monkey Face - and everything you do.

MORTALITY BITES

PART I
TODAY

Death was coming. There was nothing the old librarian could do about that.

But he could deny this monster some satisfaction.

"This will not bring the gods back," the old librarian said. "Nothing will bring them back."

The monster ran a gloved hand along the old man's cheek. "Come now, Father Dewey ... or is it just David now? You know better than anyone why they left. We disappointed them."

"We didn't disappoint them," David muttered. "The gods ... they just left. That's all. You must see that."

The monster gave a final tug on the ropes to ensure they were secure before walking past him. "No, you're wrong. We turned our backs on the old ways. We forgot the fundamental rule when appeasing the gods." The monster spoke low, absentmindedly as it browsed the library's rare-items display. It paused at the item it wanted, touching the cool glass with a light, casual finger. The monster's lips crooked up in satisfaction. "This modern world, with its iPads and unlimited data ... has forgotten that this—all of this—is because they willed it. Without the gods, we would be monkeys picking the ticks off each other's backs."

With one powerful, angry fist, it shattered the display glass and, pulling the ancient obsidian blade from its stand, the monster caressed its tip. The blade was sharp, eliciting a tiny stream of red blood where it tore into flesh. "Blood. We forgot about blood. It is the essence of true worship."

Approaching David, it held the blade aloft and muttered ancient, ritualistic words.

"You don't have to do this. It is not too late to reclaim your humanity," David said, but he knew his pleas were useless. He'd read the history books; he knew what these old rituals entailed. The fear and suffering of "that which is sacrificed"—*him*—was part of it. According to the texts, the harder the victim held on to life, the closer attention the gods paid. Mustering the last of his pride, he closed his eyes and went still.

The monster opened its eyes. Lifting the ceremonial knife high above its head, it cried out an ancient incantation that no human ear had heard in over a thousand years.

As the blade punctured his heart, David uttered a silent prayer, not for the gods to intervene—he knew that was useless—but as comfort in his last moments. After all, before he was a librarian, he was once a priest. And old habits? Well, old habits die hard.

1

TWO DAYS EARLIER

My dorm room door was open, which could mean only one of two things: I was being robbed or my roommate had finally chosen to show up.

The semester didn't start until tomorrow, but I'd arrived a week early to check out my new living digs. An old habit—necessary when you're a vampire living in secret among humans. Of course, vampires weren't a secret any longer.

And I was no longer a creature stalking the night. Though, that said, technically it *was* night, and I was returning from another one of my *scope-it-out* strolls.

Remember what I said about old habits?

One of the benefits of arriving early was getting to know the place. The other was having my dorm room all to myself.

Well, until now.

Reassuring myself that the old days of constantly being under attack were over, I walked to the threshold and looked in.

When signing up to live in the dorms, I'd had to check a box asking whether I'd be happy having an Other as a roommate. I'd checked it. I mean, ex-vampire girl here. Who am I to judge, right?

The dorm admissions board had put me on an all-girls floor

(although the floors above were full of rowdy boys), and looking inside my room, I could clearly see they had taken me at my word about living with an Other. The person unpacking wasn't human.

Not by a long shot.

She was a bit taller than me, with pointy ears and an impossibly perfect body. Athletes could work out all day and night and still not come close to the frame and muscle tone of this creature.

Other than that, she looked human enough, although no one would ever mistake her for one. Well, not unless they assumed she was twelve pies short of a baker's dozen. Humans tended to not stand completely naked in a dorm room with the door wide open. You know, modesty and all that.

It seemed my new roomie had no qualms about baring it all.

I groaned as she unpacked her peculiar possessions. Of all the Others I could have been paired with, they had to put me in a room with a member of the fae—specifically, a changeling.

A changeling who was severely messing up the feng shui vibes of our room by stapling Astroturf to our walls. (Astroturf might be the wrong word because this stuff looked like pretty *real* turf to me—mud, earthworms and all.)

Fae were obsessed with the outdoors; they drew their strength from the natural world. And changelings were of the warrior variety, which meant their homes needed to be of the earth and soil and loam so they could easily heal themselves after a battle, or some hippie crap like that.

Not that it mattered anymore. For one thing, their gods—just like everyone else's—were gone. So no more glorious battles to heal from and no more magical natural medicine. Besides, her roommate—me— wasn't fae. I was a human girl. Well, an ex-vampire human girl, but a human girl nonetheless. I definitely wouldn't appreciate finding worms and fungus on the walls.

In the center of the room, a wheelbarrow held one of those large rolls of Astroturf employed on football pitches. The changeling was using her unnaturally powerful body to unroll the bales and stick them to the walls. Mud was everywhere, and the grass—which, I was tempted to remind her, was meant to be on the ground, *horizontal*—was falling onto the floor faster than she could put it up. Clearly, this frustrated the process, but she was damn persistent; she just sprayed the walls with water from a misting bottle, trying to get the soil to clump. Drops of dirty water were streaming down the walls and—

No way … was that my brand new Louis Vuitton striped denim blazer on the floor?

I darted in, picking it up and shaking it to get the dirt off.

She turned and gave me the biggest smile, like she hadn't just destroyed our room with dirt and grass and staples.

"Oh, hello!" she said. "I was wondering when you would make your entrance."

I'm not sure what my face looked like when she said that, but I bet it was a healthy mix of incredulity and rage.

She didn't seem to notice, because she stuck out her hand and said with a lilting Irish accent, "I'm Deirdre."

I looked at her hand, not taking it. Honestly, I was more likely to bite it than shake it.

After a long, awkward moment, she retracted it, peering at her hand as if it had broken down. "The *Being Human* handbook said that humans greet one another with handshakes, but we did not. Did I do it wrong? Was I meant to wait for you to offer your hand because you were the new one to arrive? Or perhaps—"

Fae—sticklers for protocol. And this one was trying to learn *human* like an etiquette. "You didn't do it wrong," I said. "It's just that …" I gestured helplessly around me.

"Oh, yes. I got these rolls of grass from something called a 'hardware store.' Strange name, given the softness of the grass." She picked up a handful and took in a deep breath. "Perhaps you could aid me—I'm having trouble getting it to stick to the walls. You wouldn't happen to have the appropriate adhesive?"

When I shook my head, she handed me the staple gun.

I swear to the GoneGods, I thought about shooting her with it.

But instead, like a good little ex-vampire, I put it on my desk, counted to three and asked, "And why do you want it to stick to the walls?"

"Decoration," she said. Her hands pointed at the walls, and I couldn't help but notice her long, slender fingers. Staring down at my own hands, I wondered why the GoneGods hadn't seen fit to make mine so elegant. I'm big enough to admit it ... I was jealous.

"I'm pretty sure we're not allowed to staple grass to the wall," I said.

"We're not?" she said, genuinely confused.

"For one thing, we're not allowed to put holes in the walls—so that's a no to the staple gun." I had to hand it to myself: I was remarkably calm, given how angry I was. "For another, we're meant to keep our rooms clean. Which means no mud and definitely nothing that can grow mold."

"But mold isn't dirty—it's natural, and the right kinds have many healing properties. Of course, there *is* poisonous mold. I use them to line my weapons and—"

"That's a third thing we're not allowed. Weapons."

"Not even broadswords?"

She turned away and bent over. I averted my eyes before getting too good a look at her "dark side of the moon," if you know what I mean. Reaching under her bed, she pulled out a huge broadsword that would have made Braveheart's claymore seem like a toothpick in comparison. "It's more ceremonial than for actual battle. That said, I did wield this when facing off against a horde of golems. Funny story—"

"No broadswords. No grass on the wall."

"You mean no decorations at all? Even my poster?" She pointed her broadsword behind me—barely giving me time to duck out of the way—where a poster of Ryan Reynolds hung, stapled to the wall.

"Seriously?"

"Oh, yes," she said, swooning. She put a hand on her breast—or her heart, I suppose. "He's so handsome, he is almost elf-like. One day I will be Mrs. Reynolds ..."

I rolled my eyes. Fae. Of their many-faceted quirks, falling in love with an image was probably their strangest. And the love was real. At least, for them. I looked up at the poster in true sympathy. Ryan Reynolds would most likely be filing a restraining order against this changeling at some point in the future.

Then I looked at her perfect naked body and thought, *Then again, maybe not.*

Either way, that wasn't my problem right now. My problem was that this changeling was tracking dirt everywhere. "I'm sorry to keep interrupting you," I said, "but ..." I pointed at the floor around me.

She gave me a confused look.

"You're going to have to clean all this up?" I clarified.

"Really?" she said, her voice full of despair.

"I don't mind, but humans have rules and—"

"I broke them. First day here and I'm already failing." A tear rolled down her cheek. "Being mortal is hard," she said, plopping herself onto her bed and sending up a fresh shower of loose soil.

I felt for her. Really, I did, despite the ruined jacket still in my hand. I was finding mortality hard, too, and I was *human* ... well, I was *born* human, at least. But that was over three hundred years ago. I've only been re-human-ated for four years and I was finding it tough to get my mojo back.

Mojo? That's a '70s term, almost fifty years ago. I really must update my vernacular.

Still, my years as a Highland girl did give me a lot more experience at being human than she had. I sat next to her and put a hand on her shoulder, still acutely aware of her nudity. Damn, even her skin felt like it was manufactured in a lab. "Mortality does bite, Deirdre—but I'm here to help. If you have any mortality questions, just ask me. I'll steer you right."

"You will?"

"Cross my heart." I dropped my jacket back to the floor and made an X on my heart. She looked at me curiously. Before she could ask, I said, "It's a human expression. Means 'I promise.' A slightly old expression. Probably had its heyday thirty years ago, but—"

The changeling wrapped her arms around me and hugged me so

tight I struggled to breathe. Damn, she was strong, too. "Thank you, thank you, thank you!"

I'd never been hugged by a naked fae before. It was nicer than I'd expected.

After a long second, she pulled away and put her hand over her heart—a common fae salute. "Thank you, human girl. In return for your generous offer, I give you my sword arm. This is my pledge to you. This is my ..." She loosened her fist and made an X over her heart. "This is my heart-cross to you."

Oh, yay ... I'd only been here for a week and I already got a warrior fae as a protector.

Maybe college wouldn't be so bad after all.

*   *   *

I helped my changeling roommate clean up and take everything outside, which involved convincing her first to put on some clothes and then not to sniff, pick at or eat the grass as we carried it out. She really struggled with this last part; twice I caught her stuffing a handful of soil and grass into her pockets. It was slow work, but eventually we managed to get it all out the door.

Unfortunately, we didn't manage to accomplish this before some of the other girls on the floor started making fun of us. They mocked us from a safe distance (they, too, were acutely aware of Deirdre's powerful build) with comments like "Look at her *ears*" or "Eat dirt much?" Not particularly witty, but these humans were wary of picking a fight with Deirdre and, if they were totally honest with themselves, they were probably jealous of how beautiful she was.

The girls stood in little clusters and watched us. Safety in numbers, I guess—Schoolgirl Bullying 101.

Only one of the girls broke away from a cluster of her peers to help out by giving Deirdre a plot of soil that had fallen out of the wheelbarrow. She was a mousy little thing with amber hair and thick black glasses. She scurried away the second Deirdre said, "Thank you." Deirdre looked hurt.

"They'll get used to you," I said. "And as soon as some more Others show up, you won't be the only freak show on display here."

"Freak?" she asked. "What is this 'freak' you speak of?"

"You know—stranger, non-human, different. Freak."

"I see," she said, and lifted the handles of her wheelbarrow again. "We are freaks."

" 'We'? " I said, slightly offended.

"Me because I'm an Other. You because you help Others."

I sighed. "That's me, human freak at your service."

* * *

After helping Deirdre get the Astroturf out of our room, we swept up in silence. She was pretty upset, having lost all her earth and grass, but she seemed to accept that this new GoneGod World had different rules. That said, I was pretty sure I'd come home one day to her having stuffed her mattress with freshly dug dirt, but at least I got most of it out of the room for now. Small victories.

Tomorrow, I'd figure out a way to get her to give up her broadsword. After that, we'd move on to the smaller stuff, like wearing clothes and how most of nature belonged outside.

Baby steps, Kat. Baby steps.

It was late—almost midnight—and my first class started early. Best get some sleep so I could be bright-eyed and bushy-tailed for my first day of classes.

2

VAMPIRES, OTHERS, PROFESSORS
AND FOOTBALL PLAYERS

IRST CLASS BLUES—

When I was dead, all I wanted was to be alive. Now that I was human again, all I wanted to do was die. Or shrivel up and disappear. I'd never been so embarrassed in my human or vampiric life.

It all started when I walked into Professor Hayes's class and some smart aleck decided to open the drapes without any warning. Light streamed through the window and I, of course, freaked out, jumping back to avoid the sun's rays and right into Justin Truly's arms.

I may have only been scoping out the campus for a week, but you couldn't be at this college and not have heard about Justin.

Sophomore, McConnell Hall president, straight-A student and all-around hunk—and here I was in his arms, freaking out (did I mention I was freaking out?). And why? Because I was afraid of a little bit of natural light. Oh, the horror. The *HORROR!*

I knew I was a three-hundred-year-old vampire and that I should have been way cooler than I was, but I was also a nineteen-year-old girl with almost zero experience with human boys. The hormonal, boy-obsessed teenager that I never got to be was coming out with a vengeance.

"Are you OK?" Justin asked.

"Yeah. Old habits die hard, I guess."

"Old habits?" He lifted a curious eyebrow in my direction, and my heart skipped a beat.

"Yeah ..." I said, but to be honest, his question hadn't penetrated my brain. He was cute before, but that eyebrow lift ... that eyebrow lift just upgraded him from *cute* to *irresistible*.

But then I remembered where I was. More important, I remembered *who* I was. A normal human girl and not some three-hundred-year-old vampire. Well, *ex*-vampire. "Ahh, I mean ... I was daydreaming and ... the sudden appearance of the light startled me and ... well, I'm a jumper."

Justin continued his oh-so-incredibly-cute curious-eyebrow trick. "I see. First-day jitters, huh?" He ran a hand through his thick, lush black locks and I just about died—again.

Girl, I thought to myself. *Get a grip. Seriously ... you've eaten guys cuter than him.*

"I'm working on it. But like I said—"

"Old habits. Yeah, I got it." He gave me a wry smile and extended his hand. "I'm Justin."

"I know," I said, staring down at his perfectly formed fingers, as if Jesus Christ Himself were offering me a drink from the Holy Grail.

"And you are ...?"

I looked up again. "Me?"

He chuckled. "Yeah, you."

I shook his hand. "Ahh, Kat. Katrina. Kat."

"Kat. I see you are aptly named."

I gave him a curious look of my own, sans the eyebrow trick. Harder than it looked.

"You know, old habits and all. You always land on your feet."

"Feet?" I asked. "Oh, I get it. Because I'm a jumper. And a cat. Kat."

"Bingo," he said, shooting his pointy finger my way.

What did that mean? Did he just shoot me dead? Figuratively

13

speaking, of course. Or was the finger a *good* thing? Like he was acknowledging me in some kind of *affirmative, kudos* kind of way?

Being human is so hard.

Before I could think of anything to say back, I was saved by a stern, loud voice that cried out, "Will everyone take your seats? Now, please."

The class was starting. Phew.

Justin gave me an *after you* gesture and I took the nearest seat, which was way up in the auditorium, hoping he would sit next to me. But the *sophomore* football player didn't, opting instead to walk down the steps to the front row.

A dark-skinned boy a few rows in front of me gave me a thumbs-up and said in a deep foreign accent I recognized to be from West Africa (where was that? Ghana?), "Smooth, girl. Very smooth."

Yeah, smooth like sandpaper. So much for having a great first day.

* * *

Professor Hayes slammed two folders down on the table. "Why did the gods leave?"

Of all the questions I expected to be asked on my first day during my first class, this wasn't one of them. Especially because no one knew why the gods had left. Their GrandExodus happened four years ago, and scholars, philosophers, theologians and scientists alike debated what had prompted them to go. The truth was, no one knew why they left and no one would *ever* know.

"We're not gods, and therefore god logic is not something we're capable of," I muttered to myself. Sadly, far more audibly than I'd meant to.

There was a chuckle in the room.

Professor Hayes pointed in my direction and said, "Yes, a very good answer, but incomplete."

Crap, I was speaking to myself out loud again. It was something I did a lot. I don't mean to, but I guess after years of being a lone hunter and creature of the night, you get used to talking to yourself. And as for being embarrassed about it, *that* was new, too. Back in those days, I'd simply rip out the throats of anyone who dared laugh at me.

Talking out loud and no jumping at light ... two old habits I really needed get under control. *Why can't I be trying to quit smoking? At least there's a patch for that,* I thought (in my head, thankfully).

Professor Hayes smiled at me, his pudgy chipmunk cheeks squishing his eyes, making him look like the Santa Claus version of Clint Eastwood.

I stared back, not daring to say—*or* think—anything.

"You, in the back row," Professor Hayes said. "What is your name?"

"Ahh ... me?" I started, but before I could get my name out, a voice in the front row said, "Katrina. Kat for short. Careful, Professor Hayes —she's a jumper."

Justin Truly.

The auditorium chattered with muffled giggles.

Professor Hayes shot Justin a look before returning his gaze on me. "Katrina ...?" He dragged out my name like I was supposed to complete it or something.

Oh, yeah—complete it. "Darling," I said. "Katrina Darling."

"Miss Darling," the professor said. "Your answer is absolutely right. We don't know. All we do know is that the gods did exist—once—and that three days from now will mark the four-year anniversary of their departure. We also know they did not take it upon themselves to explain their behavior, instead leaving with a simple message of ...?"

He raised his hands like an orchestra conductor, and at his cue, the class sang out in harmony, *"Thank you for believing in us, but it's not enough. We're leaving. Good luck."*

The gods' last message to the world, and something every living creature heard at exactly the same time. I'd never forget where I was when I heard that voice in my head. How could I? That was the precise moment I reverted back to human. Vampire no more.

It was a strange transition, to say the least, and abrupt as all hell. I was turned when I was fifteen, and I'd spent the last three hundred years as a teenager trapped in an immortal body. An immortal body that needed blood to survive.

When the gods left, I happened to be drinking from the neck of my —*ahem*—my latest victim: a vicar I found wandering the fields alone at night in a Scottish meadow near the town of Oban. I was halfway through with him when the gods' message rang in my head. In an instant, my fangs retracted. Unfortunately for both me and the vicar, I had bitten deep enough that my front and bottom teeth gripped flesh, and as said fangs retracted, a substantial squirt of his blood shot up into my mouth and down my throat.

I pulled away and promptly—elegantly, prettily even—threw up.

Only moments earlier, the taste of blood had been something I'd craved. Now it was something I detested.

I would later find out that when they left, the gods took most of their magic with them. And me being a creature made from that very magic, I became a magicless, boring human again.

Wiping away the blood from my mouth, I thought, *"What the hell just happened?"* Evidently I'd spoken this thought aloud, as per usual, because the old vicar was nodding at my question vigorously, also experiencing his own existential crisis. His face was painted with fear and his vestments were painted with his own blood, which still streamed from his neck. But the fear on his face wasn't of me—it was fear of whatever that message was. In some odd comradery, we walked into town together, not speaking, not really acknowledging each other's existence.

As we passed an old pub, its TV blaring, we glimpsed images from the local news with the big bright letters that confirmed we weren't the only ones who had heard the message. In fact, everyone in the world heard it. The gods were gone. What we'd heard was true and my own newly grown human canines were proof of that.

But them leaving and me turning human wasn't the strangest thing to happen that night. Not by a long shot.

No, the strangest thing was the appearance of the *Others*. Seems that when the gods left, they closed all their domains, forcing mythical creatures of all religions, fables and fairy tales down to Earth. Centaurs, dragons, mermaids, nasnas, encantado—you name them— all fell down. Fairy tales raining from the sky.

And to think—prior to that day, I'd thought I was the biggest and baddest monster to roam this Earthly plane. Sometimes my arrogance astounds me.

"That's right," Professor Hayes continued. "*Thank you for believing in us, but it's not enough.* Not enough for what? To sustain them? To nurture them? To hold their interest? We'll never know. All we do know is that whatever we once gave them, whatever it was that had kept them here for millennia, was no longer enough. Or perhaps it had never been, and it took them that long to realize it."

Professor Hayes adjusted his glasses and let out a heavy sigh. "Will the Others in this classroom please stand up?"

A dust of pixies, an oni demon, a raiju, three fairies, two angels, an Incan apu and a gargoyle all stood up. I considered standing myself, but I wasn't an Other. Not anymore, at least. My current human status —and my desire to not embarrass myself in front of Justin Truly again —compelled me to remain in my seat.

But if I'm honest with myself, that wasn't the only reason I stayed seated. Truth was, I was ashamed of my past. When I think about all my victims—my *human* victims—I just want to rip out my own throat and watch myself bleed to death.

Morbid, I know. I'm working on that, too.

Besides, I used to be a freaking *demon*. Surely that counts for something in explaining my past ... umm ... indiscretions.

"Others," Professor Hayes said to those standing in the auditorium, "I welcome you to my class. As your professor, I speak for everyone here when I say that I am proud to be part of the only university on this good green Earth that accepts Others as students." He eyed those who were still seated. "For any humans who don't approve, or who distrust them, this is what I say to you—they live among us now. Deal with it. Intolerance, hatred, fear—these happen *outside* of these hallowed halls. Those destructive ideologies have no place here. Do you understand?"

The auditorium was silent.

"I said, do you understand?"

A mismatched chorus of weak *yeses* could be heard in the lecture room. Not the most resounding acknowledgment of Professor Hayes's ultimatum, but it would have to do. It had only been four years. Change takes time.

"Very good," Professor Hayes said, motioning for the Others to take their seats again. "Let's get started. History is not going to teach itself."

* * *

The rest of the class went pretty much like you'd expect a history class to go. Dates, events … yadda, yadda, yadda. Given that this class focused on the Industrial Era and I'd actually lived through that, I was surprised by how inaccurate so much of the history was. I flipped through the textbook, reading about the rise of machines that forced farmers out of the fields and into cities to find work, about overpopulation and pollution that made day-to-day life miserable.

That's not what *I* remembered.

I remembered people having more time to think, to dance, to sing. To play. Social classes were beginning to break down and, for the first time ever, the common man had a chance to do more than carry on with whatever menial profession his father had been in.

It was a good time. Not the best, but far better than what preceded it.

Not that I was going to say anything to Professor Hayes. I was a normal human girl in her late teens. Normal human girls in their late teens do not have firsthand experience of the early 1800s.

And to think that I thought this class was going to be a breeze. Now I would have to learn everything they claimed happened and use it to replace everything I knew had *actually* happened.

Arrgh!

The bell rang and everyone started to pack up and leave. I purposely took my time, hoping Justin Truly would come my way and talk to me. This time I would be more suave. Cool as ice. Act more my age. I'd be the bee's knees—no, that's not right. That was human vernacular in the 1920s. This was the new millennium, the

GoneGod World. Unfortunately, I had lived through a ton of those eras, each with its own particular and peculiar vernacular—plus, I had a *deeeep* love for '80s and '90s TV—so I wasn't really hip to modern slang. Yet.

What I did know was that in this era, humans didn't use words like *bee's knees, groovy* or *rockn'*. And one wasn't *in* or *down with it* anymore.

Modern humans were now saying things like *GoneGodDamn!* and *Empty Heaven*. I'd even heard some idiot say *Hellelujah!* Probably thought he was being clever or something.

That's what I needed to be—a modern human. But not all of me needed to be modern. I could use some of what I'd learned to lure him in. One thing I learned when stalking prey was that you didn't wait for Justin to show up. You just happened to be in his path when he did.

I pretended to be engrossed in the class textbook. When he passed, he'd stop and say "Hi," or maybe something cooler, like "Hey." I'd lift a casual finger as if to say *Give me a minute* before looking up as if unaware who had been standing there.

Yeah—that was what a modern human looked like. Calculatedly casual.

Besides, I didn't need to be too strategic, because—not to sound full of myself—I was cute. Not gorgeous, mind you, but cute. I had a kind of Reese-Witherspoon-in-*Legally-Blonde* or Sarah-Michelle-Gellar-in-*Buffy* vibe going for me. I had a cute, confident—yet somehow helpless—aura that I'd cultivated over the centuries of being a vampire.

I had to. It was how I hunted.

During that time, I had two main shticks to lure in my prey. The first one I called *Cute and Helpless*, and it went like this: "Oh my, Mister Big-and-Strong, it is dark outside and I'm scared. Do you mind walking me home?" That was good when I wanted a quick meal without all the fuss of my prey screaming and running.

The second technique was reserved for when I was in a playful mood: *Cute and Terrified*. In that routine, I'd find some dark alley or secluded place and start screaming for dear life. Eventually, some macho guy would come running and, well, let's just say there was some screaming and running on his part. I'd play cat-and-mouse with him for a bit before, you know … to work up an appetite.

I'll admit it: I was a real bitch back then. But part of me being human again was atoning for all the bad I did when I was the monster who went bump in the night.

* * *

The other students shuffled out of the class, but no Justin. No worries —he had sat in the front of the class, so it made sense it would take him a while to get to me. But when the auditorium went quiet, I dared a glance and saw that everyone was gone. Everyone including Professor Hayes. I was totally alone except for the kid from Africa, who stared at me from two rows down.

Evidently, I wasn't cute enough for Justin to stop and talk to me.

Disappointed, I packed my stuff and stood up. As I did, the kid— who was totally checking me out, by the way, and not in a *cute* kind of way, but in a *creepy-stalker* way—kept his eyes on me. It felt like he was looking *through* me, rather than *at* me.

I couldn't take it anymore. I was human, but I wasn't helpless. I knew things—like where all the major arteries were and which nerves crippled your prey versus the ones that absolutely paralyzed them. Plus, in my travels, I had studied a variety of martial arts. A lot. I figured I was probably one of only a handful of humans with such a wide range of styles, and I'd had hundreds of years to practice them. But although I knew what I was capable of, my heart still raced when I met his gaze and said in the harshest tone I could muster, "What?"

The guy didn't flinch. He just sniffed the air and said, "You should have stood up."

3
HISTORY IS FOR THE HYENAS

"*W*hat? When?" I said, looking the kid right in the eyes. Creepy guys tended to divert their gaze when challenged.

This creepy guy didn't. He simply kept staring. "You know when."

"I don't know what you're talking about. I'm just a girl. A *human* girl."

"Sure you are."

"I am," I repeated as I slung my bag over my shoulder, and realizing that this guy took creepy to whole new level, I opted to leave the room as fast as I could.

* * *

Out in the main hall, I saw Justin mulling about with his McConnell Hall buddies. They jokingly called themselves the Omega Omega Omega (O^3 for short) Bros. Their little gang were legends on campus for throwing the biggest and baddest parties.

One of the things I learned while scoping out the place was that they got their name because the Latin letter Omega is mistakenly associated with the Apocalypse. You know—God saying He was the

Alpha and Omega and all that. And given that the departure of the gods was an apocalypse of sorts, I guess they were tripling down on the rhetoric. I kinda wanted to tell them that Omega didn't mean *the end*, but rather the concept of God being the Alpha and Omega was to give Him a cyclical, renewing nature. You know, circle-of-life kind of stuff. The gods leaving made that Biblical quote kind of meaningless, anyway. But these guys were teenagers on the cusp of adulthood—they were far more interested in the cool factor of the name than anything else. Who was I to burst their bubble?

Besides—Justin made the O³s cool. He made everything cool.

The O³ Bros were standing in a line, handing out flyers alongside an Incan apu who was in the history class with us. They were jostling each other, seeming to be having a good time. Professor Hayes's warning that we should all get along turned out to be unnecessary. Here were three humans and an Incan apu—an Other belonging to a religion that was now ancient history—and they were getting on just fine.

I tried to position myself so that Justin would hand me one of the flyers, but instead I was intercepted by the apu. Apus were Incan nature spirits and were usually associated with a place—a forest, a river, even a town. These spirits were defenders. If you ever caused trouble in a place protected by one of these guys, you were in for one hell of a fight.

Up close the apu looked like a normal human except for one, eerie difference: he was made of rock. I don't mean like the Thing in *Fantastic Four*, nor do I mean he was carved from stone like a gargoyle. His skin was the color of a cave floor, like it was made from slate, with tiny ridges that swooped along his forearm, giving it a weathered look.

But that wasn't the strangest or most captivating part of him. No, that was reserved for his eyes. It is said that the eyes are windows to the soul—but this apu's eyes were more like actual windows to the outside. Like I was sitting in a tunnel looking outside to the clear blue, endless sky. Beautiful, eerie, intense.

The apu handed me a flyer and our fingers briefly touched. His skin didn't only look like a rock, it felt like it, too. Hard, rigid—like touching a moving stone. What's more, he had dust on his skin, and as I took the flyer, a little bit of sand rolled down its front. This guy flaked sand like some humans flaked dandruff.

I read the flyer:

O^3 cordially invites you to
THE END OF THE WORLD
When the gods left, they started an apocalypse.
We aim to finish it.

The O^3 party—the first big party of the semester—was two days from now, on the anniversary of the gods' GrandExodus.

And I was invited.

"So—you in?" His voice had an echo to it, like he was talking in a cave or something. It was a bit unsettling, because generally when one echo was present, all the ambient sounds echoed, too. But here, it was only him. The shuffle of students milling about was perfectly normal.

"Your voice ..." I said.

He smiled, like his voice was something that got him a lot of attention from ... well ... the girls. I guess we all have a shtick—and his was to impress the impressionable with his resonance. "I'm a cave apu—caves have echoes, hence my voice," he reverberated. "Actually, I was one of the twelve sacred apus of Cusco." When I gave him a blank look, he followed up with, "Cusco was the capital of the Incan Empire in the fifteenth century."

"Ahh, so a big deal. Five hundred years ago."

"Oh, yeah—very big deal five hundred years ago," he chuckled. Sticking out his hand, he said, "I'm Sal."

"Oddly normal name for a guy like you, wouldn't you say?"

He gave me a shy smile and said, "My real name's Salkantay, as in the highest peak in the Vilcabamba mountain region. You know—the Peruvian Andes."

I nodded. I'd been there. Granted, that was 180 years ago, but still, I'd seen the place.

Sal closed his sky-like eyes for just a second, but I swear it felt like night had suddenly fallen. Then, when he opened them, a light sky with big puffy clouds returned. "Anyway," he said, almost embarrassed, "the guys thought it was best to give me a more, ahhh, human name. You see Nate over there—he came up with 'Sal.' " He pointed at the shortest of the Bros, a kid with brown hair cut in a buzz, and I could see genuine affection in those impossibly beautiful eyes of his. "I think they meant it to be ironic. Something so average for someone who looks so different. But I can tell you that I am very honored to be given such a normal name. It means they don't see me as an Other, but as a friend."

"He's right. The fact that those guys teased him by giving him such a boring name means they accepted him as one of them."

"Boring name?"

Damn it—talking out loud again. I could feel my cheeks flush with embarrassment. " 'Sal' certainly isn't Algernon or Constantine ... so, yeah, boring."

"Yeah, but these days I'll take boring over the alternative."

"I suppose," I said.

"So, the party," he said, tapping the flyer in my hands and sending another wave of sand down the paper. "It's this Friday. Will you come?"

"Maybe ..." I said, throwing in as much coyness as I could.

Evidently, the coyness didn't take, because he said, "Great, see you then," and went on to hand another flyer to three girls behind me.

I folded the flyer and put it in my purse. I waved at Justin. He gave me a subtle nod as he continued to play-wrestle with Nate without losing stride. If anything were to happen between Justin and me, it wouldn't be now. And so, taking that as my cue, I headed out to the main campus, where I hesitated at the threshold. My foot nervously hovered just behind the line where the shade met the light. Like I said —old habits do die hard.

I took a deep breath and stepped into the light. Even though I knew I was human, I still breathed a sigh of relief that I didn't burst into a ball of flames.

Yay, me!

4

BEGGARS EVIDENTLY CAN BE CHOOSERS

& EVEN COOL KIDS CAN BE AWKWARD

*T*he sun didn't disintegrate me—so at least one thing was going my way today. I know it's irrational for me to be scared of natural light, but you have to understand that I was a vampire one minute and then a human the next, while fang-deep in some vicar's neck. It was like someone had flipped a switch. *On—vampire. Off—human.*

If the *vampire* switch could be switched off, for all I knew it could be switched back on just as suddenly. And if I happened to be outside … great balls of flame *à la moi!*

I really should start walking around with an umbrella.

Just when that thought occurred to me, my eyes were drawn to the large oak tree in the center of the quad, beside that GoneGods-awful statue of the university founder, where I spotted three human hockey players tormenting some homeless guy. Except, given his unearthly pale white skin and ruby-red eyes, this homeless man clearly wasn't a man at all. He was an Other. A type of Other I'd never seen before.

I was pretty hip to Others—able to recognize most of them on sight, thank you very much—but this one eluded me. He didn't even have any of the telltale signs of what religion or folklore he belonged to. There was no wispy mustache so typical of Chinese traditions, no protruding lower-jaw tusks most Japanese demons had and no animalistic and oddly two-dimensional attributes you found in most Egyptian Others.

Instead, he—I *think* he was a "he"—wore baggy white pants that were scuffed and dirty but when clean would have matched his impossibly white skin. He had a long-sleeve dirty white shirt on that looked more like undergarments than a proper top. His hair was also the same white as his skin, and because the coloring matched so perfectly, it looked more like strands of skin on his head than actual dead-skin-cells-and-keratin hair. In fact, the only thing he had on him that wasn't white was his cane—a crooked oak staff that looked too flimsy to actually support someone's body weight. Not that he had much weight to him. He was absolutely emaciated. The term *skin-and-bones* didn't do him justice. It was more like skin-*sundried*-on-bones. Poor guy must've been dying of hunger.

The lead human—a largish guy with black hair and a nose that looked like it had been broken, set wrong, then broken again—kicked the homeless guy and shouted, "Get out of here, you freak!"

A second human—a smaller, skinny guy with blond hair tied back in a ponytail that will totally embarrass him when he is older and looks back at pictures of himself—said, "Bad enough they let these freaks enroll in the school, but now we have to put up with their vagrants, too. Oh, *hell* no!" He emphasized this by spitting on the Other.

That was the last straw. I ran down the steps of the building, over to the tree, and grabbed the skinny guy. Using a move I learned from a judo master in Kyoto some 150 years ago, I pulled him back so that he fell over his own feet and tumbled backward.

I put myself between the other two humans and the Other and, summoning a real gem that I probably got from *Degrassi: The Next Generation* or *Beverly Hills, 90210*, said, "Why don't you pick on someone your own size?" Stupid really, because *I* was picking a fight with them, and all three of these guys were way bigger than me. I really had to work on my vernacular.

The biggest one pointed at me and said, "Get out of our way, little girl. Otherwise—"

I grabbed his finger and twisted. This wasn't a move from any martial art I'd learned, but something I'd used against my little brother when I was human—three hundred years ago, sure, but it still did the trick. The big guy cried out in pain and tried to punch me with his free hand. I pulled back and kicked his shin, forcing his left leg out and his right knee down. Then, when we were about eye level, I punched him. Hard. In the nose.

There was a sickening *crunch*! Given how little power my punches usually packed—since I became human, at least—I must've been right about his nose being broken before. The thing crumpled like a paper cup. He dropped to the ground, blood pouring out of him.

His friend, a slightly smaller version of him, sized me up and decided to charge.

Employing a move I learned from an aikido master in San Francisco (about forty years ago, if you're keeping track), I used his own momentum against him, guiding his body into the wall behind me. He hit face-first and dropped to his knees.

The ponytail guy stood up, saw his downed buddies and ran. The other two managed to collect themselves from the grass, the bigger guy still clutching his blood-gushing nose, and followed their friend. I half expected them to say something like "You haven't seen the last of us!" or "We'll get you, just you wait and see!" but I didn't get any of those cliché gems as they ran away.

Looking around to see if there were any other threats, I saw that a bunch of people were looking at me from all around the quad. And not just students. Professors, Others—heck, even Justin Truly was watching from the steps of the Arts building across the quad. Suddenly, several of them started clapping, then hooting, then *cheering*.

I guess standing up for this Other was a … good thing?

I realized something, blushing as my peers and professors clapped me on the back. I may not be smooth or the bee's knees or even the cat's pajamas, but I was heroic ... and in this new GoneGod World, that seemed to count for a lot.

* * *

After I gave a few bows and enthusiastic thumbs-up, people went about their usual business again. I turned to the homeless Other, fished through my bag and pulled out a granola bar that had been sitting at its bottom for weeks. I handed it to the guy, half expecting him to eat it cellophane and all.

But he didn't. Instead, he read the wrapper in detail and, breathing a sigh of relief, handed the unopened granola bar back. "Thank you," he said.

"You can have it. I mean—eat it." I tried to hand it back.

The strange Other looked at me with a confused expression on his face. "I already did." He groaned. "Not very good."

"OK ..." I said with trepidation. I had to admit, though, that this guy looked a little better after having read the package. I was beginning to wonder if this weird Other didn't eat granola. Or oats. Or whatever this supposed nature bar was made of. Made sense—after all, you would no more give a rabbit steak than a lion a carrot. For some Others, eating mortal food was deadly. Maybe that's why this poor guy was so emaciated. Human food just didn't work for him.

"So, no granola?"

He shook his head. "No granola," he whispered.

"So what can you eat?"

"The truth?" The poor guy was so weak that he was having trouble speaking.

"Yeah, the truth," I said, trying to throw in as much empathy as I could. It was possible that this kind of Other ate something very unappealing to humans. Kappa ate algae. Pixies considered maggots a delicacy. And succubae ate— Well, succubae drew nourishment from sex. Besides, who was I to judge? For three hundred years I lived entirely off of human blood. Let she who is without sin cast the first stone. Stones firmly in pocket.

Being a bona fide *Homo sapiens* and law-abiding citizen meant there was no way I could have sustained myself on pig and cow blood. Believe me, I had tried and it nearly killed me. But that's another story. As for these newly mortal Others, algae, maggots and sex weren't something you could get at your local grocery store or farmer's market, so kappa learned to eat kale, pixies substituted nuts for maggots and succubae bought naughty mags for a quick snack. It must have been a rough existence, and rarely a day goes by that I don't silently thank the GoneGods for taking their magic and turning me human again.

I looked down at him with an understanding smile, waiting for his answer, but the strange Other just groaned in response. OK—so be it. I took a mental picture of the guy, determined to figure out what he did eat, and said, "I'll be back tomorrow. With real food. I promise."

His eyes glistened with gratitude.

* * *

I looked at my watch and saw that it was quarter past one. My next class started in fifteen minutes—no real chance to go to the library now. Especially because I had no idea where my next class was. I was really, really, really starting to regret not going to the orientation meet-up, but it was at eight in the morning—and I hadn't seen that ungodly hour in over three hundred years.

My map was a mess—I didn't know where I was and there was no convenient "You are here" mark, no conveniently labeled "Oak Tree Quad." Just when I was resigning myself to missing my second class on my first day, a hand snatched the map out of my hands.

"Hey," I said, getting ready to kick someone in the shins … until I saw who the perpetrator was. My demeanor immediately changed and I tried not to swoon too hard. "Hey, Justin."

"That was pretty amazing of you," he said.

"What was?"

"How you kicked those guys' asses. Total jerks, by the way."

"Oh, that. They were being bullies. I hate bullies."

"Me, too."

"Oh, great. Something we have in common," I meant to think—but wound up saying out loud. *Girl, get a grip!*

"Yeah, we do, I suppose," he said, eyeing me curiously. "I take it that outside of being scared of light, you're also a bit quirky, too."

"You could say that." I blushed. "Is that a bad thing?"

"No," he said, "I like quirky. And I like cats ... so we're good here."

I felt my blush darken three shades.

"So—where are you going?"

"Going?" I said in an absentminded tone.

He held up the map.

"Oh, yeah—class. I've got Literary Theory in Alternative Cultures now, but I have no idea where I'm going."

"That will be over here." He pointed at a building on the map. "Here—I'll walk you." He held out his arm like gentlemen used to do when inviting dames to dance in the 1800s. How retro of him.

"Cute and helpless—works every time."

He looked at me, his eyebrow doing that dance again. "Excuse me?"

"Oh, nothing."

I took his arm, and as I did, his O^3 Bros sang out from the top of the hill: "Justin and Weird Girl sitting in a tree!" Neither of us said anything, but we both looked up and smiled. This would have been a perfect moment ... had it not been for the kid from West Africa staring down at me from behind the others on the hill.

That guy was really starting to give me the creeps.

5

LIBRARIES DON'T JUST HAVE BOOKS, YOU KNOW

*M*y second class went a lot smoother than my first. No mishaps with cute football players, no speaking my thoughts aloud and drawing the whole class's attention to me. And no jumping at the sight of light. I'm particularly proud of that last one.

With class over, I checked my schedule: no more classes today. In fact, my next class wasn't until 3:00 p.m. the next day. Sheesh … university life. I had fifteen hours of lectures and that was it. What was a girl supposed to do with all this free time?

I hefted the monstrosity my professor called a textbook, considered all the articles that were supplemental material (plus, let's not forget the five essays in this class alone) and realized that if I wanted to do well here, I knew exactly how I was supposed to use the rest of my time.

Reading, writing … and not sleeping.

It was day one and already I knew that all the parties, boys and fun that *Animal House*, the *Van Wilder* series and *Revenge of the Nerds* promised were lies.

As they say in my native Scotland: nae bother. I wanted to do well. I *needed* to do well.

I will do well here, I told myself, *even if it kills me.*

Time to hit the books. After, that was, I kept my promise to that pale white Other and figured out what he ate.

Either way, it was off to the library for me.

* * *

Finding the library was a lot easier than finding my last class. For one thing, it was the biggest building on campus, and for another, you could see all those books through the windows. No map necessary.

I walked inside and approached the directory. In the old days—and mind you, by "old days" I mean five years ago, just before the Others came—you couldn't find an entire library section dedicated solely to mythical creatures. That stuff was usually distributed between sections: the Classics housed information about the Greeks and Romans; the Asian Studies section had all the stuff about Japanese, Chinese, Indian and other Asian countries and religions; and if your library had a children's section (this university, surprisingly, did not), that's where you'd find most other fairy tales.

But these days, all those books were collected into one department, aptly called Other Studies.

Bingo, I thought. Or did I say it out loud?

* * *

The Other Studies Library was so big that it had its own building. An old converted church that sat on the main campus right next to the Arts Building. It was easily half a football field in size, three floors high, the upper levels had wraparound balconies looking out into the center of the library, where all the study tables were located. Dozens of bookshelves lined both sides of the study area and, from my angle, I could see that the upper level held several dozen more sets of shelves.

I'd never seen so many books in one place.

I didn't know what Heaven was like—and now that it's closed, I guess I never will. But I imagined it to be this place.

When I was a vampire, I spent a lot of time in libraries. This was before television, remember, and I was really into reading, devouring every book I could get my hands on. I did also eat the occasional bookworm—I don't know what it was, but humans who were into reading tasted sweet, like sucking on a mango.

So, walking into the place, my heels lightly tapping on old, worn marble, its soft tones echoing off wooden shelves that housed well-loved books—well, for the first time since I'd become a university student, I felt at home. I closed my eyes, lifted my hands from my side and spread out my fingers so I could absorb this place all the more.

"Of course," I thought, *"I'm not really absorbing anything, but it still feels good to try to soak it all in and—"*

"Ahem."

I opened my eyes to see several people sitting at the study tables staring at me. A few were suppressing giggles, but most just gawked at me, like I was a freak or something. And they were right—I was talking out loud again, and, according to TV and movies, only freaks and the criminally insane talked to themselves.

There was a second "Ahem" and I turned to see an old man standing near an old oak desk. He was staring at me over the rim of his reading glasses, his bald head reflecting the lights overhead. He did up the top button of his jacket and pointed a weathered finger at a sign.

PLEASE BE RESPECTFUL OF THOSE STUDYING.

"Sorry," I whispered, and walked to the back of the room, now very conscious of the tapping my heels made with every step.

* * *

When I made it to the back of the library, I saw that books weren't the only things this massive library housed. Toward the back of the main floor were numerous rows of display cases. I walked over and found that they housed hundreds of artifacts. Some of them I recognized: an old Bleeder vampires pricked their victims with when they wanted to slowly drain them overnight; a spiked silver collar mages used to control their pet werewolves; an obsidian ceremonial blade once used for human sacrifice; a Horn of Abundance that the desert-wandering nasnas blew to summon their nightly feasts.

There were even several of King Solomon's rings, each of their rubies trapping a protective spirit that would do the wearer's bidding. I wondered if the rings still possessed the trapped spirits ... not that it mattered. It would take powerful magic to release them—and powerful magic was in short supply these days.

But the artifacts and rings were just the tip of the mythical-artifacts iceberg. Most of this stuff I had no idea about, but this much was clear—a lot of Others donated a lot of their stuff to this place.

I walked among the artifacts—some impossibly old, others once supremely magical in nature—in awe until I wove my way to the back display, where I saw something I had never expected to see again in my life. Right there in a display case that hung on the back wall was a full Scottish uniform from the late 1800s, complete with tartan, ghillie brogues, sporran, kilt pin and dirk. I don't think it would have stood out so much if it wasn't for the fact that it was my clan's tartan—when I had a clan to call my own.

But it was more than just recognizing the old crisscrossed bands of color that made up my clan's pattern. You see, at the foot of the display sat a faceplate I hadn't seen in centuries. The faceplate facade was designed to cover the wearer's face from hairline to chin, and because it was made of iron, it also protected the wearer from attacks. That thing was built for battle. Not that you would assume so by looking at it. It was fashioned to look like a baby's face, complete with rosy cheeks and an innocent smile that a fool would interpret as friendly. I recognized the mask immediately. It was my *father's* ... and it was what he wore the night he hunted me down in the Grey Friar's abbey.

The night I killed him.

As I took a step closer to the display case, still lost in thought, I suddenly sensed a presence behind me. *What the—?*

"Can I help you with anything?"

I turned. It was just the old librarian, standing directly behind me. Either the guy had the prowess of a cat or I had been too distracted to sense him there—probably the latter, from the look of him. Either way, he scared the bejesus out of me.

"What?" I yelped.

He lifted a finger over his lips, then in a whisper repeated, "Can I help you with anything?"

He was so close I could smell the mint coolness of a lozenge still on his breath. He also had that old-man smell to him, but not an *I'm overmedicated, sick and waiting to die* kind of smell. This smell said, *This body has seen and done a lot in its years, and those experiences have been soaked into my bones.* Hey, don't judge me—as a vampire, smell was very important to me. Like a wine connoisseur's nose, mine told me a lot about the person I was about to eat.

Old habits, and all that.

"No talking, remember?" I mouthed, giving him a serious look.

At this, he let out a muted laugh, and a warm smile overtook his features. "There are degrees to which a rule can be bent without breaking it. If we are respectful, no one will mind our whispers."

"Oh, OK," I mouthed, and turned back to the display.

He walked up to the hanging uniform and adjusted his glasses as he took a closer look. "Ahh … this is an old tartan, old, indeed. It was donated to the library by the Divine Cherubs—an ancient order of vampire hunters. It belongs to their founder, one Eoghan McMahon from the clan—"

"Blane."

He lifted a curious eyebrow. "Correct. But that is not a common clan, and the crest had been modified to represent his mission to vanquish demons. How did you …?"

"I'm half-Scottish. My dad was really into our clan's history. I grew up learning all the patterns."

"I see," he said, still wearing a skeptical look. "Well, then you have heard of the great Eoghan McMahon ... It is believed he was the first Scottish vampire hunter, and the man who ultimately created the Order of the Divine Cherub." He walked up to the display and pointed at the mask. "A baby's face. Or, more to the point—a cherub's face. Hence the order's name. Legend has it they wore masks like this when hunting. Angels to exorcise demons, you see."

I sighed in grief, but the old librarian must have interpreted my exhalation as that of a bored teenager. "Don't dismiss them too quickly," he said. "After all, we now know that vampires and demons are real. The Order of the Divine Cherub fought them in the shadows for centuries." The old man tapped the glass, then gave a low chuckle. "Of course, now they mostly meet in log cabins, drink whiskey and talk about the good old days. But make no mistake—back in said good old days, they were a force to be reckoned with."

I know that better than most, I thought—and did not speak aloud, thankfully.

The old librarian pointed at my father's tartan. "Eoghan McMahon," he said, reverence in his voice. "Legend has it his daughter was turned and—"

"—then his daughter turned his wife ..." *Turning my mom was stupid. As in ... Stupidest. Thing. I. Ever. Did,* I thought, making sure it was in my head.

But when I turned, I was so hurt that my father insisted on hunting his little demon daughter down that I did the most passive-aggressive thing I could think of: I turned my mother, too (not my best move, because, well, mothers were one thing ... but homicidal, vindictive mothers with supernatural strength and predatory instincts determined to kill you were another thing altogether).

Still, losing the love of his life to his only daughter hurt him very deeply. And that was exactly what vampire Katrina McMahon was trying to do.

"And in his grief and rage, he dedicated his life to eliminating the vampire kind from the Earth. Hunting daughter and wife, alike. Yep—I know all about it," I said with a sad familiarity.

I walked over to the display in hopes that this old librarian wouldn't see the tears welling up in my eyes. Not that I had much hope of that; I was recalling the single most painful memory of my long, long life and I doubt I was able to hide my emotions when I recalled, "A lifetime spent avenging his daughter, only to be taken down by her in Edinburgh on the night of Hogmanay."

The librarian nodded, his look of skepticism returned. "Scotland's New Year's. He did disappear then, never to be seen or heard from again … but there is no record of what happened that night. As far as the historians know, he simply vanished. Of course, rumors abounded, but …" He took a step forward so he could get a good look at me. "Is there something you can contribute to his history? Something his descendants know but has not necessarily been adopted into canon?"

"Ahh, no," I lied, chippering up my voice as much as I could. "It was just what my dad said happened. You know—a romantic ending to the vampire hunter. That kind of stuff."

"Your father sounds like a poet."

"You have no idea," I said, looking at the tartan. When I was a vampire, the sight of his mask had stirred no emotion in me. But now that I was human again … I had to fight to hold in the tears. I don't think I would have been able to do it, except for the old librarian. I couldn't risk him suspecting what I was.

So I took in a deep breath and, summoning all the cold-hearted steel I could find in my soul, asked, "How did you get this?"

"It was donated, just as all the artifacts here were," the old librarian said. "Most of this came from Others who now live among us—little keepsakes that were on their person when the gods left. And some of it had been passed down generation to generation, humans who had brushes with the creatures behind the veil. But now that the veil is gone, I guess they no longer felt the need to hold on to these artifacts and donated them to this display. Perhaps it helped them move on with their new lives."

"I see. But you don't know who donated this particular tartan, do you? So I can tell my father," I quickly added. The truth was, I was curious—I had no siblings, and as for my mom …

The old librarian looked at the display's accompanying plaque. "It doesn't say. I can look it up for you, but I'll have to dig into the archives. I would be willing to do that for you later tonight."

"That would be grand," I said.

"Grand? That word was antiquated when *I* was a child."

I blushed. "What can I say? I watch a lot of old movies."

"I see," he said. "Now that we have had our little chat, perhaps you can answer my original question."

"What's that?"

"Is there anything I can help you with?"

I told the old librarian about the strange, pale Other—what he looked like, what he wore—and as I spoke, the elderly man picked up book after book, leafing through them as he tried to find the creature I described. After he'd pulled down several books from their shelves, the old librarian put his finger on a page from an old leather-bound tome and asked, "Pale white, you said?"

"Yep—I've seen ghosts with more color."

"You said that he had a cane with him?"

"Not a very good one. It looked like it would crack under his weight—even if he only weighs sixty pounds soaking wet."

"So it might not be a cane at all."

"Possibly, but he holds on to it like it's the only thing he has left in this world. Whatever it is, he values it."

The librarian turned his book around and showed me a picture of a pale white Other riding a pale white horse, bow in hand. "Is it possible that the staff isn't a staff at all, but rather an unstrung bow?"

I took the book from him to study the image more closely. The creature on the horse was white, but unlike the creature I'd helped, this being was proud, strong and slightly overweight. "I guess," I said uncertainly.

Coming around to look at the book with me, the librarian said,

"Mergen. A Turkish being of wisdom. I believe we've found your Other."

"But it says here that Mergen was a god."

"So?"

"So the gods are gone."

"Ahh. Therein lies the rub—the gods are gone. But not all their *avatars* are."

"Excuse me?"

"Avatars—Earthly representations of the gods. Most gods did not have avatars, but the ones that did often left theirs behind. After all, why would they need an Earthly representative when there was no guarantee that where they were going would have an Earth?"

"I know what an avatar is, I've seen the movie. So these avatars, are they like the gods' Seconds?"

"Now it is my turn to say, 'Excuse me?' "

I laughed softly. I was starting to like this old guy. "In a duel, when you were either too scared or too busy to participate yourself, you sent in your Second. This guy is the god Mergen's Second."

"Exactly. A Second—that term is quite archaic, especially in this context."

"Ahh, my dad—"

"The romantic."

"Yeah, him. He was also a history buff. You know, one of those guys who'd dress up like a knight on the weekends and go ..."

The librarian nodded, smiling. "LARPing. Live action role-playing. I know the type."

I diverted my gaze back to the book, pretending to be embarrassed rather than a liar. I wasn't used to lying so much. If I ever needed to get out of a tight situation before, I usually just ripped off someone's head and had a quick snack.

I looked at the image of the proud being riding that magnificent horse. "How sad."

"How sad, indeed," the librarian echoed. I looked up, confused by his response. He gave me a knowing smile and said, "How sad that a creature, once-upon-a-time proud and important, be reduced to a beggar, unable to defend himself against three scared human teenagers."

"Unable ... or unwilling," I said.

"Hmm?" He lifted an old, gray eyebrow. "Elaborate."

"This Other's bow tells us he's a warrior, and myth tells us he's a sage—in other words, the wise warrior. And what do all wise warriors have in common? They only fight when there are no other options. Mergen knows that if he retaliates against those bullies, he will only scare them more. So they'll come back with more force, and it will never end. He also knows he can't kill them. Not in the GoneGod World. That would only cause more fear, more hatred."

"So he takes the beating."

"Because he is wise enough to know that, in the long run, that is his best option."

"That hardly seems fair," the librarian said. "And not every Other agrees. If you watch the news, we see plenty of Others fighting back."

"Which is good for the individual, but not the group. Overall, they're making it worse for other Others. The Others have to first prove they're not a threat before we can start talking about what's *fair.*"

"Indeed," the librarian sighed. "Fairness will only come to them after they endure much that is not fair. So if an Other cannot fight back using their fists and weapons, how then do they fight back? After all, they cannot exist as humanity's whipping dogs forever."

"No, they can't," I agreed.

"So?"

"I don't know what to tell this old librarian," I thought. "It's not like I have all the answers. Besides, what he's asking doesn't have an answer. Not yet. The Others will have to wait and see what happens and—"

"I disagree," he said, eyeing me curiously. "And I don't appreciate being called 'this old librarian.'"

Crap, I'd been talking out loud again.

"Then again—I *am* old, and a librarian ..."

"Ahh, I'm sorry. I meant to *think* that, not say it."

"Doesn't make me less old."

I chuckled at this, glad he wasn't taking what I'd said too seriously. "Granted. But I don't know your name, and the 'old' thing ... well, I tend to think out loud. A lot, and not on purpose. Sorry about that. It's a bad habit that I'm working on—"

"Please don't," he said, his eyes serious. "Those thoughts you *accidently* share are always the honest ones. This world needs more people saying what they think and thinking what they say. And as for my name: Old Librarian will do ... for now." He put out his hand.

I had never thought about it that way before, but he was right. Over my three hundred years, I had spent a lot of time without any living person in sight. Talking to myself was always a way to combat the loneliness. But what came out tended to upset me, and I'd have long, bitter arguments—my voice unwaveringly honest, versus my rationalizing, compromising inner thoughts.

I looked at his hand for a long moment before taking it in mine. "Nice to meet you, Old Librarian."

"And nice to meet you, Peculiar Girl. Now that those pleasantries are out of the way, I wish to disagree with your earlier point. 'Wait and see' is *not* all they can do. Far from it."

"I don't see what else they *can* do. Not without causing a lot of harm to themselves."

"True, change is hard. Still, there are ways to minimize the ire they will inevitably draw on themselves as they work for a brighter future. Organized protest and passive resistance, to name a couple."

"Like the suffragettes and civil rights movements. Like Gandhi. Mandela."

"Yes, but those are grand examples. Back when I ran my congregation, I saw many brave men and women who fought for equal rights in small but very meaningful ways. There were plenty of Rosa Parkses refusing to go to the back of the bus who never made it to the news. Plenty of brave souls who stood up to bullying without ever being recognized for their bravery. And no single one of them invoked change. But the sum of their deeds ... that is another story altogether."

I didn't know what he meant by that, but I nodded anyway. I'd mull over his words later. Turning back to the book, I said, "If you're right and he is Mergen's avatar, we still don't know what he eats. All it says is that he's Turkish and that he's the deity of Wisdom and Abundance."

"That's a start, isn't it?"

"I guess." I pulled my purse over my shoulder. I supposed figuring out what that poor Other ate would take some time. "Thank you," I said, and started for the door. Then I stopped, with one more burning question I had to ask. "You referred to your congregation. So, you were a priest before, you know, you became the Old Librarian?" I said, smiling.

He stared at me over the rims of his glasses. "Who said I am no longer a priest?"

"You did. You referred to your congregation in the past tense."

"Indeed—but only because the flock has thinned after God's GrandExodus. But His absence doesn't mean that I don't have faith anymore. Quite the opposite, in fact. I now have *proof* that the God I devoted my life to is real."

"And gone," I said, regretting my words instantly. I was being rude.

He nodded at this, giving me a patient smile. "And gone—you are quite correct. But my faith was not contingent on His presence before He left. That has not changed just because I know He is gone."

"So why *have* it? Faith. Sounds like an unnecessary burden."

"Perhaps—but then again, our past defines our future, no matter how hard we try to bury it."

I looked over at my father's tartan. "Maybe. But some of that stuff is best left in the past."

"Perhaps. But then again, perhaps not. You have a keen mind. Tell me, do you have a campus job, Miss …?"

"I thought we weren't doing names, Old Librarian."

"I promise to call you Peculiar Girl, no matter what your name is. I ask for different reasons." He paused, waiting expectantly.

I obliged. "Darling. Katrina Darling."

"What a pretty real name you have, Peculiar Girl," he said, smirking but not unkindly. "You have a keen mind, and your banter is something I think I would enjoy. Do you have a job? Or rather, would you like one?"

"A job?"

"I need someone to help me catalog and organize this place. The pay is abysmal and the job can take you into the wee hours of the night—but you will have unfettered access to all this." He gestured around him to the shelves of books bursting with knowledge and the display cases packed with history. "And perhaps we will have time to debate the past and contemplate the future while enjoying the present."

That would be nice, I thought. "I like working nights," I finally said. "I'm kind of an insomniac."

"Very well then. I shall put your name down as the new assistant librarian. Officially it is ten hours a week, which means I will only pay you for a fraction of the time you'll be working."

"Great," I said, wondering if *great* was the right response when basically agreeing to be an indentured slave.

"Great, indeed. Address?"

"Gardner Hall. Room 001."

He wrote that down on a little notepad he'd pulled from his breast pocket and said, "You start tomorrow."

Then he stuck out his hand. I shook it, and headed to the door. At the threshold, I stopped. I wanted to turn around and tell him how he had made this scared freshman feel welcome and how much I appreciated having not only a job but a bit of a purpose in my new life. But instead, all I mustered was an awkward "Ahh ... thanks," before leaving.

If I had known that would be the last time I'd see Old Librarian alive, I would have maybe tried to say something a little more meaningful.

And I would have asked him for his real name.

End of Part 1

PART II
INTERMISSION

He stands perfectly still in the moonlit night, near the statue of the university founder. He is under the canopy of the large oak tree and is facing east because, although it is near midnight, the moon has yet to fully rise. That will happen in the coming hour. For now, he stands and waits.

He waits for the moon.

And for it to call to him.

In the old days, he would have assumed the form of a hyena with his fellow pack members. They would have all faced west, just as he is now, together waiting for the moon to reach its apex. Then they would have sung out to her in pitch-perfect unison, thanking her for her lunar light under which they would hunt.

They would praise her beauty and love her for being the mother of night.

Then the pack would let the frenzy of the hunt take over.

But that was years ago, before the gods left. Now that the gods are gone, his pack has disbanded. Some embraced their humanity. Some left the old lands to seek new opportunities in this new GoneGod World. Some refused to accept the change and still go out nightly to praise the moon goddess. And some could not handle the change, choosing forever-lasting death over this new life.

But Egya—Egya is different. A hybrid among his fellow hyenas. He chose to both embrace his humanity and honor his past. The gods may be gone—but the moon goddess still hangs above him. Of that much he is sure.

* * *

The moon is nearing her apex—in moments she will have fully risen. Egya is preparing his howl, summoning the low, guttural hum within.

It is good that he is alone in this field. His roar is mighty and it would scare any human unfortunate enough to happen by.

But just as he is about to unleash his howl, he sniffs someone approaching.

He does not need to see her to know who she is: the Other pretending to be a human. The one who lost her magic, just like him. Moving with the silence of an experienced predator, he stalks around the tree, out of her sight. There he stands perfectly still, tracking her movements not with sight and only partially with hearing.

He mostly tracks her with smell. The gods may have taken his hyena form from him, but they did not take his superior sense of smell—not all of it, at least.

She stops by the statue, some trace of her former instinct telling her someone is near. But she embraces her human side far too much, and she suppresses her instincts, choosing to ignore them and move on, rather than stay and explore possible dangers.

Egya lets out a low, disapproving growl. Her past—her Otherness —it is a gift. A gift she denies.

And this angers the former were-hyena.

This angers him greatly.

6

DAYSTALKER, NIGHTWALKER

*I*t was dusk when I left the Old Librarian, and so I engaged in another one of my quirks from my vampire days. The long walk in the dark. You know, the whole creature of the night wandering around at night. Cliché, I know, but it was my jam.

My jam? Did that refer to jam as in a band jamming, or jam on toast? Or both. And when was my jam *in*? Argh, I needed elocution lessons. Actually I needed slang lessons, but somehow I didn't think the university offered those.

Looking at my wristwatch I saw that I had been wandering around for quite some time. It was almost midnight. But I didn't feel like going home. Not yet. But where could you go at this time of night on a Tuesday?

Most of the campus would be closed. The only place still open was Gerts, the campus bar, and given that it was the first day of classes and a school night, I guessed even Gerts wouldn't be open for much longer. Besides, I didn't feel like a drink even though I *was* of the legal age according to the mortal law in the Quebec province. Here you only needed to be eighteen to drink. Younger than most places. *It's the French influence*, I guessed.

Regardless, I was nineteen.

By now, I'm sure you would correct me on that one: I was actually over three hundred years old. But the way I figured it, I was—biologically speaking—still only nineteen. I was turned at fifteen, so I figured that when I returned to being human again, I would start aging from that point. I'd been human for four years since the GrandExodus—so four plus fifteen. Nineteen.

My math skills were impeccable. I was sure to make the dean's list.

Anyway, that's how I saw it, but I wasn't sure how the rest of the world saw it. You see, ever since the Others came, mortal law had been challenged on multiple levels. Legal definitions had to be broadened and bastardized and reevaluated to include Earth's newest residents.

But society was still too busy dealing with angels, minotaurs, wendigos, avatars and all sorts of OnceImmortals. We half-breeds were largely ignored—partly because we were technically human, but mostly because we never went into the limelight. After centuries of hiding from humans, we were pretty good at confining ourselves to the darkness.

* * *

I walked down the hill toward the university's main campus and took a deep breath. Autumn was on its way, which, in Montreal, meant that real cold was coming. Montreal was a university town with four major universities within its city limits. I went to McGill—the best of the bunch (or at least that's what other McGill students say).

Montreal itself wasn't a bad place to live. European feel with North American sensibility; friendly people, not too smug; lots of bars, clubs and other places for frustrated locals to let off some steam. When I was a vampire, this would have been ideal hunting grounds. As a student, Montreal was ideal party grounds. Funny how the two go hand in hand.

But partying and hunting aside, what made Montreal special was that it was built on (and around) an inactive volcano. I wished it were a *dead* volcano, but it wasn't. Not that anyone was worried, though.

Montreal's volcano hadn't shown any sign of activity since I was born —yeah, three centuries ago. That was a good indicator that it was safe enough, right?

Then again …

Four years ago, mythical creatures barely showed any activity on Earth either.

And look where we were now.

But still, a volcano was a volcano, and the locals, several decades ago, had decided to hedge their it-won't-erupt bets by putting a cross at its very top. A Christian, neon-lit, bigger-than-an-upright-bus, vampire-burning cross.

And *this* was the city I chose to move to?

What's more—I actually lived *on* the volcano. If you walked up the hill, past the Royal Vic Hospital, past the McGill football stadium, you entered McGill University dorm territory. If this volcano erupted soon, we freshmen would be the first victims. Seems fitting, if you think about it.

McConnell, Molson, Gardner and Douglas Halls all sat about halfway up the hill, along with a large circular cafeteria that was cutting-edge architectural design … in the 1950s. I lived in Gardner— the dorm that was the absolute closest you could find to that beacon of a cross.

Every time I trekked up the hill, staring at the cross, I would just think to myself that moving here had been some inner penitence or something. You don't spend three centuries as a murderous immortal demon without developing your inner masochist.

I walked onto the main campus field, which never seemed to close —too many late-night studies—and passed by James McGill's statue. The Scotsman explorer was a short, stout man, holding his pioneer hat against the wind, cane planted firmly on the ground in one hand, the other pointing straight ahead. It wasn't a grand statue or anything. The guy was my height, and I was born in eighteenth-century Scotland—we were a lot shorter than today's average human.

I gave my fellow Highlander a pat on the head. Immediately, the hair on the back of my neck stood up. In the past, that was what happened when danger or potential prey was nearby, like a vampire's sixth sense. Maybe late-night studiers were finally going home, or perhaps two lovebirds were making out in the moonlight.

But I saw no moonlight lovers, no late-night studiers walking home, nobody. In fact, I noticed for the first time that everything around me was eerily dark—no lights, no noise, all the buildings long abandoned.

I take that back. There was one light on the main floor of the Other Studies Library. I guess my senses were on the fritz.

Oh, well.

I peered closer at the Other Studies building. Seems the Old Librarian was still working, and I wondered if he'd be up for a visit. Maybe he would finally be able to tell me how he got my father's tartan.

"Besides," I thought (out loud, probably), *"I'm his newest employee ... and technically it is tomorrow."*

* * *

The library had one of those old wooden church doors. From the front, I couldn't see inside—all the large windows were on the sides of the building, with only two slender, stained-glass displays flanking the entrance.

I tried the door. Locked.

I jogged back to where I'd been to look up at the window again, but there wasn't enough light to make out what was happening inside. At this point, I usually would have just given up and called it a night, but I wasn't especially looking forward to finding Deirdre naked in our dorm again (I swear! I wasn't!), and something about this whole thing was starting to make me feel uneasy. That vampire sixth sense again, maybe? I jogged to the front door once more and, pulling back on the iron knocker just within reach, I knocked and waited.

Nothing.

I was about to give up, when I felt the hairs on the back of my neck stand up. When I was a predator, those hairs had saved me more than once. Up until now, I had assumed they were a part of my vampiric nature. Either I had carried over some of that nature with me or that tingly feeling had been my human part all along.

Either way, I had learned to trust that instinct. The door was locked, nobody was answering the knocker ... I scrutinized every inch of the door and the surrounding facade, until I spotted a mail flap near the bottom of the door. I pushed it open and peered inside. Two desk lamps were lit in the study area, but from this angle, their light only revealed a couple of cushy armchairs and an empty fireplace. Nothing of interest.

But I could smell something.

A smell I knew very well.

Human blood.

7

VAMPIRES AREN'T ONLY HUMANS

*H*uman blood. Unmistakable … I should know. I'd only spent the last few centuries guzzling it down like a camel in a desert. A … vampire camel? Whatever. Poor simile, but you get the point.

Smelling it as a human was completely different than drinking it as a vampire. As a vampire, the smell excited me, intoxicated me—drove me mad with insatiable desire. But as a human, the smell of blood made me retch, and the thought of tasting the crimson liquid made my stomach twist with nausea.

Get over it, girl, I thought as I tried to find a way into the library. *It's probably nothing too serious.* I tried to comfort myself with the thought that the Old Librarian had merely fallen and hit his head. That the smell of blood came from a head wound, not a gaping throat or severed carotid artery. A few stitches and a concussion would be the worst that he'd suffer.

But the smell was way too strong for that … and as much as I tried to lie to myself that he'd be fine, I'd been involved in enough death to know better.

The Old Librarian was dead. The part of me that was still vampire knew that.

The human part of me, on the other hand, still clung on to hope.

I pulled at the door handle again—no good. I'd need a battering ram to get through this heavy wooden door. If only I still had my vampiric strength. But what I lacked in strength, I made up for in smallness. The windows that ran along the side of the door were narrow, barely the size of a dinner plate. But I could work with that. Now all I needed was something to smash the window with. I ran to the path leading up to the library and picked up a heavy stone lining the flower bed. Rushing back to the door, I hefted the stone and smashed it through the window.

Then, taking off my Hermes jacket—still muddy from Deirdre's home decor—I wrapped it around my arm and cleared the rest of the glass, silently lamenting the lacerations the leather suffered from the process. I'd definitely have to buy a new one now. Good thing I had money—and lots of it. Three hundred years of antique collecting and compound interest tends to do that.

Glass cleared, I sucked in my breath and shimmied through. I made it in—barely—with only my butt and my chest getting squished as I did. Evidently, those parts of me were a bit wider than a dinner plate.

Inside I wasted no more time. I let my nose guide me to the back of the library's main floor, near to where the artifacts were kept—but even without that sickly smell as my guide, a part of me knew this was where I'd find the old man.

As I got closer, the smell of blood became stronger and stronger. Turning the corner, I braced myself for what I thought I'd see.

But what I saw was much, much worse.

* * *

The Old Librarian was strung up on the heavy, oak bookshelves closest to the display cases. His hands were literally nailed to the thick shelves. His feet, positioned one in front of the other, were held together by a thick metal spike, which had been driven through them.

He hung in a crucified position on that shelf. I might have thought his killer was imitating the classic Christ crucifixion ... if it weren't for the stuff on the floor.

Like some Egyptian mummification process interrupted, four canopic jars had been arranged in front of him, each holding a different organ. His small intestines sat on a silver tray, his large intestines on a gold one. And as for his blood—that had meticulously been drained from his body, into large clay pots. Very little of it had been spilled on the floor. His murderer had been precise.

My eyes were drawn back up to his body. His chest cavity had been torn open and I only saw an empty hole where his heart should have been.

I groaned ... but this was not the worst part by far.

From the expression on his face, I knew that he had been awake while he was being ripped apart.

"Oh, Old Librarian," I whispered. "Why didn't you scream for help? Why didn't I hear you?"

The answer came when I looked down and saw that his tongue lay on a cloth right in front of us both. The cloth was wet, not only with blood but also mucus and saliva, which meant that the monster responsible took the time to stuff his mouth with that cloth to muffle his screams. The monster most likely cut out the Old Librarian's tongue after he died.

This didn't make sense. Too much was going on here. The crucifixion, the ceremonial draining of blood, the way the organs were distributed in the four jars ... the tongue on a cloth. It was like he was killed by a bunch of monsters from a dozen different horror movies.

I tried desperately to keep my composure. I'd played my part in quite a lot of killing. Some for fun—most of it to survive. But I had never been a part of something such as this. Say what you will about vampires—we never did this to our victims.

I turned away, having taken in as much of the scene as I dared. With my back to him, I now faced the cases housing an array of Other artifacts. Several of the display cases, I now noticed, were broken and empty. I didn't need to turn around to know they had been used in the sick killing behind me. I couldn't recall exactly which ones had been in those now-empty cases, but I breathed a sigh of relief when I saw one that wasn't missing—my father's old Scottish dirk.

His display case stood untouched.

As I stared at my father's weapons, I considered my next move. What happened here was recent, maybe even minutes from completion, which meant the killer or killers couldn't have gotten far. I could hunt them down—after all, I was pretty good at that. But I was also human now. What would a human do? A human would call the police. It would take ages for them to get down here, and the trail would probably be cold by then. But they had modern forensics and—

Crunch.

Coming from the front of the library, the unmistakable sound of a foot crunching down on glass.

The monster was still in here ... and had accidently stepped on some of the glass I'd smashed when breaking into the library—which meant it (I can only assume something capable of committing such a horrible crime was an it) was trying to escape.

Looking at the old Scottish dirk, I knew what I had to do.

I may no longer be a vampire.

But that didn't mean I wasn't still a killer.

8

DIRKS AND LIPSTICK

The monster stopped moving, evidently waiting to see if I had heard the glass beneath its boots ... or claws, or ... whatever passed as its feet. This monster was playing it cautious, which meant that it wanted to escape without incident.

That wasn't going to happen.

Even though the old rush of the hunt came surging through me, I fought the urge and stood perfectly still, pretending not to have heard my prey. Then I listened.

Faint breath came from the front of the library.

I slowly counted in my head, waiting, listening. In a minute, I'd make my move and either it would attack me or run. Either way, whatever I did would have to put me in the best position to take it down. I thought about the Old Librarian. He had been frail, weak— certainly not trained like I was. He wouldn't have put up much of a fight. That meant I couldn't gauge my opponent's strength on what I knew.

What I *did* know was that it was at least strong enough to string the Old Librarian up, which put it in the class of a big and strong human at the very least. I also knew that it contained the resolve and constitution to brutally tear apart a living creature—to *crucify* an innocent old man and harvest his friggin' organs—without sympathy or mercy. This most likely meant that when I did engage with it, the monster wouldn't hesitate to put me down.

But I also knew the Old Librarian was a good man who had treated me kindly. This knowledge alone was enough to lead me to one final conclusion.

This monster was going to die ...

... and I was going to be the one to make that happen.

The minute was up. The monster hadn't made another move, so it was my turn. I darted forward to my father's display case and smashed the glass with my elbow. I reached in and very nearly managed to get my hand on the dirk before powerful hands pulled me back and threw me across the room. Of course, ever the college freshman looking to impress (or at least fit in as *human*), I just *had* to go out in my Versace dove-white silk blouse. On smooth marble floor such as this, my blouse was like a sled. I slid across the floor until I hit the front door—with my head.

So much for this monster being as strong as a large human male. More like a frigging bull, or an elephant. Maybe a bull elephant.

I probably would have spent the next minute on the floor, groaning in pain—if it weren't for the large figure bounding from above. It would have crushed me under its weight, but I regained my wits and rolled under one of the large study desks.

A black claw ripped the table back. I rolled under another table. The claw ripped away this table and I rolled beneath the next. Then another.

This perverse game of musical chairs—well, tables—wouldn't last forever. I knew I needed to get a weapon if I wanted a chance at fighting this thing, which meant I needed to put more distance between us than a few layers of lacquered wood.

I faked rolling beneath another desk, then darted between two shelves instead, using them as cover. Lucky move—the monster was wider than the space between the shelves, and as it charged, its weight pushed them apart, causing them to knock over like dominos in two directions.

Good … just what I wanted to happen. This creature was a predator—which meant that it hunted using sight, smell, and noise. The clambering shelves and tumbling books would cover any sound I made, and all the book dust puffing into the air would mask my scent. Which only left it sight—and, as I've said before, what I lacked in strength, I totally made up in smallness.

When the shelves tumbled down, they didn't fall flat, but rather tipped onto one another like drunks, creating little tunnels beneath where one shelf rested on another. Those gaps were as wide as the shelf's width—which was thankfully about twice the width of a dinner plate. Perfect for me (including my butt and chest, this time).

I crawled through the opening and listened. When I was sure the monster was on the other side of the shelves, scratching about and searching for me, I ducked into the next makeshift tunnel, then the next. Ultimate Hide-and-Go-Seek.

The monster stalked the aisles, occasionally leaping on the toppled shelves and bringing them splintering deeper into one another. But it couldn't find me. And from the sounds it was making, I could tell it was getting frustrated.

I smiled, vindicated. *This is for the Old Librarian, you bastard. Run, while you still can.*

A little cocky on my part, I know. That was the vampire in me. Either way, the monster didn't take its chance to run. It kept methodically leaping from one shelf to another, snarling.

OK—have it your way.

Slowly, carefully, I made my way to the last row and peered around. Across the aisle, I could see the Old Librarian still strung up. I don't know if it was seeing him there or if it was my fight-or-flight instincts kicking in, but either way, the brave, stupid part of me took over. I darted out of the makeshift passageway and, leaping from display case to display case—

I jumped for my father's dirk and shield.

After all these years, it took scant moments to fit the ancient artifacts in my grip, like well-oiled hinges. Weapon in hand, I turned to face the monster. For the first time I got a good look at it.

GoneGodDamn—if I had seen it earlier, I might have acted smarter. And way less brave.

* * *

The thing looked like an honest-to-the-GoneGods bulldog—if, that was, the bulldog were the size of a Highland coo, had fire-yellow eyes and snorted friggin' steam out of its nose.

Oh well ... no use in crying over spilled milk, I thought as I held out the dirk.

It slammed two of its massive claws on the ground, gouging into the marble as it prepared to charge. I did the same, minus the marble-gouging. Given my stature, it was more like doing the two-step. Still, it was the best retort I had. If I could snort steam, I would've.

It sniffed. I growled.

It roared. I screamed back defiantly.

And with the pre-fight ceremony out of the way, we charged at each other.

* * *

It was big and fast, but I had something it didn't.

A silk blouse.

At the last second I dove into a baseball player's slide and under it, thrusting my long dagger upwards. A fountain of lava-hot blood poured out of its belly. If it wasn't for my shield, I probably would have been burned to death. Luckily I was able to divert the stream as I rolled out from under it. Turning, I immediately abandoned my shield as it literally burst into flames, its wooden frame consumed by this thing's blood.

The thing about Others—they don't bleed red. Ogres bleed green, dwarves a dirt brown; angels bleed actual light and pixies dust. But fire? Only one being I knew bled fire—a jinni. God made jinn from smokeless fire. I guess that explained the flickering yellow eyes this thing had.

It reared up onto its hind legs, still spilling blood from its midsection, seeking to crush me under its weight. I rolled to the right, expecting it to try and step to the right and crush me, but instead, it swiveled to the left.

I had all of one second to consider why it would do that when its tail swiped across the floor (did I say this thing looked like a bulldog? Its tail was more like that of a dragon's, spikes and all) and hit me hard in the chest, causing me to drop my dirk. I was pushed to the side and before I could tumble out of the way, it pinned me to the side of the wall. Its big flat-nosed face was an inch away from mine and it was bearing its fangs, long, pointy bastards dripping oily fire. I could tell it was relishing the moment before it would bite my head off—literally.

It had me, and without a weapon or any gods to hear my prayers, I didn't have a hope in Hell of getting out of this alive.

Except we weren't in Hell—and hope was a fickle bitch that liked to wait until the last second to swoop in. This time, she took the form of my fellow classmate, the weird African guy, who leapt on the monster's back and—what the hell?—bit down on the thing's neck.

"Kid—I don't know what you're trying to do, but I'm pretty sure that wasn't the best—" I started to think (out loud—good to know I could still rely on my quirks in life-and-death situations) when the kid reared his head back and spat out a clump of the monster's neck, fiery blood and all.

The monster reeled back, howling in agony. Steam and lava poured out of its wound and I just managed to roll out of its waning grip.

"Holy crap, kid," I said, running for my dirk.

The kid—who had been knocked off the beast's back—tumbled in my direction, dabbing at his blistering lips. "Holy Hell! That was hot!"

"Jinni, kid. Jinn. They bleed fire."

"Apparently. And, for the record, my name is not *kid*. It is Egya-Boi Awooner of the Fante."

"And I'm Connor MacLeod of Clan MacLeod," I said.

Egya gave me a curious look and I managed to say, "What? Not a *Highlander* fan?"

Before he could answer, the monster, who had managed to pick itself up from the steaming blood-slick floor, resumed its attack. It raked its claws at us, forcing us to split apart. The creature, unsure which target to pursue, chased after me—and not because it was a "Ladies first" kind of monster. No, there was something else going on.

Not that I could ponder that particular mystery *now*.

Now I had to avoid its massive claws. I ran to the far end of the library, seeking to draw it to the display, hoping against hope that I'd be able to find something, anything to use against it. Maybe a spear or some kind of anti-jinni weapon.

Wishful thinking, but stranger things have happened ... like giant bulldog-faced, dragon-tailed, lava-spewing monsters chasing you through a college library on a Friday night.

I ran, and as fast as I was, this thing was faster. Where the hell was Egya? I couldn't hear him, and a shiver ran down my spine. If Egya ducked out of the fight, I was done for. Maybe that bite of lava had been more than he'd bargained for.

I kept running for the displays, but it involved a lot of obstacle-course dodging of the mess I'd made with the toppling shelves. Before I could get close, the creature flipped a shelf full of several heavy books over, toppling it at my feet and tripping me over.

I fell on my stomach and quickly turned so that I was lying flat on my back. The creature came close, getting ready to bear down on me. Pointing the tip of my sword straight up, I was preparing for the old stab-and-roll maneuver when I heard a howl. Egya jumped from the viewing balcony on the second floor, straight onto the creature's back.

Egya had learned his lesson: he didn't bite the thing. This time he stabbed it with something I couldn't quite see from my vantage point. No matter. Stab as if my life depended on it, Egya!

Taking my cue from its howl, I thrust my dirk into the nape of its still-bleeding neck and then twisted my body as hard as I could to the right, gripping my sword with all the human strength I had in me—and maybe any vampiric strength still left deep down.

My sword stuck in its molten skin. Despite the heat, I continued with as much pressure as I could. I felt my sword travel through its skin another inch, then two more, and with one last effort, I managed to slash through the thing's throat—ripping a hole in it the size of the library's book-return slot.

The monster tried to scream, but without a throat, all that came out was a low, guttural hiss as it collapsed to the ground in its own molten blood.

"Damn. Remind me not to get on your bad side," Egya said, climbing off the creature's back.

I ignored him, walking around it slowly. According to Islam, God created two types of humanity: one from mud—humans; and the other from smokeless fire—the jinn. The jinn were like us, complete with different races, ethnicities and geopolitical alliances. And although this creature had all the telltale signs of being jinn, it was more animal than sentient being. Something didn't feel right.

As I examined him, my foot hit something hard by its front left paw. Looking down, I saw my father's cherub mask on the ground, its innocent face staring up at me out of the fiery blood. The irony wasn't lost on me—here I was fighting an evil demon to avenge the death of my friend … How many demons had my father vanquished in my name? Too many to count, I suspected.

Gingerly picking up the mask, I slipped it in my slightly torn jacket pocket. *Arrgh, is thing was beyond repair*, I lamented (in my head).

Egya had been watching me the whole time. Seeing his gaze, I was just about to say "Let's get out of here before the police show up," when I heard a voice yell out, "Hold it right there!"

Two flashlights shined in our eyes. Behind the glaring light, I saw two figures approach with guns drawn.

"Oh, great—campus security's here. Great timing, morons."

The voice behind the lights barked, "What did you say?"

Talking out loud again. I really, really had to stop that.

9

HUMAN SECURITY SECURING

*F*irst the campus security came, then the cops, then the local news and finally the coroner. Not that we saw any of that. Deirdre told me later. Word had gotten to the dorms what had happened and many of the students, including her, went down to see what happened.

Egya and I were interviewed at the scene—in handcuffs—and after our statement was taken down and taken down again by every cop determined to crack the truth out of us, we were whisked away to the local police precinct in a police car, sirens ringing through the night air and drawing unwanted attention to us. Already a ton of students were out; I wanted to curl up in a fetal position at the floor of the cruiser from embarrassment and shame—and loss. Twenty-four hours had yet to pass and already I was the freak who jumps at light, gets into fights with hockey players and gets arrested for murder. The murder of the one person I'd managed to make friends with.

At least no one can say I don't make a first impression.

The nearest precinct was about a mile away. Once we made it inside, I noted that there was a disproportionate number of Others in handcuffs. Made sense—Others were the easily distinguishable minority and seeing them in chains just proved to me that the world didn't change that much just because the gods left.

Once our prints were taken (our hands had to be washed and treated for burns first), Egya and I were separated. I was guided to a room with a desk and one-way mirror. Presumably so was Egya.

Then I waited.

And waited.

And waited some more.

I'd been in similar situations before, so I knew the drill. They wanted us to get nervous, because nervous people talked. The trouble with me and waiting was that, as an insomniac, former vampire who hunted in the night, when I wasn't talking to myself, I was really good at sitting perfectly still for long periods of time. It's not that I went asleep or anything. I just kind of shut off. Meditation on overdrive. When I'd go into that state as a vampire, I'd actually stop breathing. As a human, I couldn't do that, of course, but my breaths were low and shallow and infrequent. Not sure if this skill would have real world applications, but one thing I noticed happened when I did this was I made other humans really nervous. And in situations like this, I got a bit of sick pleasure out of that.

The door flung open, and the way the detective—a woman with a gray suit and an olive button-up shirt—burst in, I knew she'd seen me through the one-way mirror and thought I'd had a seizure or something.

The movement caused me to turn. When I animated, I could see the detective visibly relax.

"What the hell are you doing?" she asked.

"Meditating," I answered honestly.

"Meditating?"

"Well, kind of. I play old movies in my head. It relaxes me."

She raised one eyebrow. "Huh?"

"This time I was screening *An American Werewolf in London*—the original, not the remake in Paris. I was playing the scene where they were walking back to the pub and—"

"And why were you playing that movie in particular?"

It was my turn to raise an eyebrow. "Because ... did you see that thing? I kind of feel like I was attacked by a werewolf myself. I'm sort of wondering if I'm going to turn into a giant bulldog with hot, lava-like blood."

"I see," the detective said, taking off her glasses and sitting down across from me. "And you do this to—what?—relax? Why do you need to relax?"

I gave the detective a wry smile. This wasn't the first time I had found myself in an interrogation room for killing something—or killing some*one*. Caught plenty of times when I was a vampire. This was, however, the first time I was in a place like this as a human—*and* for killing an Other.

As a vampire, I'd wait until it got really late and bite my way out. As a human, I would need another tack. Luckily, I was one of those psychological Hannibal Lecter–type killer vampires (as opposed to the hack-and-slash kind) and was used to playing mind games. Unhinging the detective with my meditation trick was a start. Better she was nervous than me ... but still, if I was going to get out of here, I needed to be very careful what I said and didn't say.

So I considered her question before replying evenly, "How many people, innocent or guilty, get put in a room like this and *don't* need to relax?" I gave subtle emphasis to the word *innocent*.

"You've got a point," the detective said. She stuck out her hand. "Detective Sarah Wilcox. And you are?"

"Katrina Darling, but you know that already, from my statement. I suspect that you know a lot more than that, too."

She nodded. "OK—yes—I've run your name through the databases. So can you imagine what came back in your file?"

I froze. It was possible she had uncovered that I was an ex-vampire. I had done my best to hide my tracks. I paid a lot to get myself a long-form birth certificate, I fabricated a death certificate for a fake father who'd died prematurely from a heart attack ... I even had my bogus dad set up a trust fund for me—an accumulation of my assets collected over the centuries of long life.

In my human story, Dad was a diplomat and we'd moved around a lot—that way I could have fewer ties and less (read: zero) schoolmates to remember me. Hell, I even set up a Facebook page with doctored photos of me doing human activities in the sun as a little girl (thank the GoneGods for stock photography and Photoshop).

Still, humans—the AlwaysMortals, that is—were paranoid about Others, even former Others, and had created a registry for beings like me to sign. There was even an amnesty program for vampires, were-wolves, ghouls and zombies—expunging us from any legal recourse for the murders we committed when we were an Other.

But ... I never did. And technically speaking, that meant I was breaking the law.

Detective Wilcox turned the file around. It was thin, with only a couple pages visible. Evidently, she wasn't going to tell me what she'd found without me asking. GoneGodDamn it—any upper hand I had with my meditation trick would be gone if I asked. Still, I had to know.

I sighed inwardly. "What?"

"Nothing," she said with a smirk—she knew she'd just won this battle of wills. "But you were awfully nervous, given how little there is about you."

"Well, you know—it's my first time talking to a real detective," I lied.

"Sure, sure. These are unusual circumstances." She pointed at the mirror, and a few seconds later a cop walked in with a file and my bag. "But we had expected more, even for a young first-year like yourself."

I shrugged. "I moved around a lot and my dad was a very private person. Before he died, that is."

"Yes, your file mentioned that. Sorry for your loss."

I nodded. She was the second person today to offer me condolences for a man who died before the *Titanic* sank.

"OK, Ms. Darling, there are a few other things we need to know." Detective Wilcox turned the file back to her, extracted an envelope, pulled out some photos and spread them out in front of me.

I had expected the photographs to be of the crime scene—the Old Librarian strung up, his organs displayed like pastry in a bakery—but instead, they were pictures of the Old Librarian alive, healthy and smiling. Then there were photos of him and me speaking beside the display cases. And finally, a photo of me standing outside the library at night—it must have been taken just before I tried to break in. Barely two hours ago.

"These certainly tell a story," she said.

"How did you get those?"

"CCTV—there are cameras all over campus."

"Hmph." I picked up the photo of the Old Librarian and looked at it. My voice softened. "Did he suffer?"

Detective Wilcox narrowed her eyes. She hadn't been expecting that question. Not at this point, at least. "Excuse me?"

"When he was killed—did he suffer?" I wasn't playing a mind game with the detective; this wasn't a trick like the meditation. I really wanted to know if he had suffered in the end.

"I would like to answer your question, but before I do, I need to know ... what makes you ask that?"

"It's just that the way he was killed—it was ritualistic, or psychotic, or both. Point is, it was preplanned. His killer wanted to hang him that way, wanted to cut him open that way. Wanted to pull out his organs that way. Either the killer was doing that because he—"

"He?"

"He, she, it—whatever," I said, annoyed with myself for the assumption the killer was a boy (this was the GoneGod World—girls were just as capable as boys of being killers). That and accidently hinting that I might know something when I didn't. "My point is ... either the Old Librarian suffering was part of this or it wasn't. And given how much blood and gore and dismemberment there was ... why didn't someone hear his screams? Someone like, oh, I dunno, the police?"

The detective glared at me, but I kept going.

"Maybe the killer put him asleep before doing what ... ahh, *it* ... did."

She folded her arms. "That's quite the astute observation for someone with a file thinner than a rice cake."

I shrugged. "I watch a lot of TV."

The detective raised one eyebrow.

"A lot."

"OK," she said, "tell you what: I'll answer your question if you answer mine."

"You really going to blackmail me into speaking to you over the question of whether or not my friend suffered when he died?"

Detective Wilcox paused at this. "No, I suppose not. From blood splatter, an examination of his body and blood work that measured the presence of adrenaline and other elements, our best guess is that the initial cuts were done with him fully awake, but as soon as those preliminary steps were taken, the killer drugged him. After that, he probably didn't feel much when he, she or *it* really started to get into it."

Really started to get into it. Well, that's one way of describing what had happened.

"So you don't know who the killer is?" I said.

Detective Wilcox pursed her lips, putting on her best poker face, but after centuries of playing mind games myself, I knew the answer. She had no idea who the killer was.

"Nothing on the cameras, then?" I asked.

Lips pursed. Poker face. Nothing.

"What about the Other that Egya and I killed? He could have been acting alone, right?"

She shook her head. "No, he wasn't. But we'll get to him in a moment."

She emptied the contents of my bag onto the table. There was lip gloss, a vintage wallet containing forty measly bucks, my student ID, my debit card and credit card, my phone, my dorm keys and the O^3 flyer.

Oh, and my father's cherub mask. They'd confiscated that from my jacket pocket pretty quickly.

She picked up the flyer. "O^3 is still at it, eh?"

"Excuse me?" I narrowed my eyes.

"O^3—the party organizers. My cousin's one of them."

"Oh? Which one?"

She paused for a moment like she was considering not telling me, before she finally said, "Nate."

"Yeah, I know him. Sort of. More like I know *of* him. And from what I know—nice guy."

"You have no idea." She dropped the flyer, looking at my other stuff. "Very well, then, let's start by you telling me what this is." She picked up the mask.

"Give that back," I said, lunging forward. I immediately regretted doing that—just another instance where I was giving the detective the advantage, probably even playing right into her hands—but seeing my father's mask in this cop's said hands stirred some old rage in me. I was simultaneously scared by the image of the Divine Cherub and upset that another person dared touch my father's most prized possession.

"Hold on, missy," she said, pulling back. "So this is important to you, huh? What is it?"

"Sun protector," I said. "I wear it to keep all those nasty UV rays off my face."

"Cute," she said. She dropped it on the table, just out of my reach.

I don't know why I'm being difficult. I guess I'm just scared, I thought.

"Makes sense. You just saw a dead body. I've been on the force for years and I'm still not used to it."

"Yeah, you're probably right," I said out loud—on purpose this time.

"So, the mask? Care to elaborate?"

"It's … very old. An antique, you might say." *A family heirloom, you might say,* I was careful to think silently.

"And … *not* a sun protector, I take it."

I shook my head. "No—just something my dad gave me. It's been in our family for generations," I admitted, glossing over the fact that I had stolen it from the library.

The detective looked at me expectantly. I was lying to her by omitting certain facts, but it wasn't like I could just come out and say that I stole the mask from the library, but it wasn't technically *stealing* because it really *was* a family heirloom.

So I did what I always did in situations like this: I kept lying.

Fake it till you make it. That was basically the ex-Other motto.

"I brought the mask with me to university because ..."

"Because ...?"

I shrugged, assuming a carefully guarded look of sadness. "It reminds me of Da' ... and I'm homesick."

She looked up at me, putting down the pen.

"The mask—it was something my father really loved and, well, I guess I wanted to have something to remember him by."

Detective Wilcox stared at me for a long time before finally nodding and saying, "OK—you're free to go." She handed me a card. "If you think of anything else, please call me directly."

"What?" I took the card, staring at it blankly, a bit surprised this was it. "Nothing else? No questions about what I saw, felt ... did?"

"The officer on the scene already got your statement. If we need anything else from you, I'll be sure to contact you."

"So that's it? I'm free to go?"

"That is what I said."

I didn't move.

Detective Wilcox gave me a curious look. She gestured at the mask. "We know that didn't have anything to do with the librarian's murder. What's more, forensics is pretty advanced these days and we didn't find a single hair strand, fabric fiber, fingerprint or DNA sample of yours on the scene."

"Really? You got that already?"

She sighed. "No. But I don't *expect* to find anything. We have campus security footage that clearly shows you leaving your dorm and going for a walk at the time of the murder. Because of those little cameras everywhere, violating your privacy rights but aiding in allowing your freedom to *have* privacy rights, you have an airtight alibi."

"Oh?" I said. "Oh! Well ... good thing I'm not that private of a person anyway."

The detective gave me a suspicious look, then shook her head. She was clearly tired. "Unless there is a reason I should be arresting you ... you are free to go." She pointed at the door.

I know that was what I wanted, but being let go so easily really boiled my blood. For one thing, I was the first person on the scene, and the junior cop who took my statement had barely scratched the surface of what I could tell them. Granted, a lot of what I knew stemmed from my experience as a vampire, and I wanted to protect that secret as best I could—but still! Couldn't this self-important detective recognize an asset when she saw one?

But that wasn't what really upset me. No, what engulfed my recently returned soul in flame was that she was letting me walk after I killed an Other. A living, breathing Other.

"Is Other life so worthless that you could literally kill *one of them and not go to jail? Or—even if I killed him in self-defense—can't the authorities at least investigate with more than a passing interest? Last I checked, killing someone in self-defense at least requires an investigation. I should be calling my lawyer. I should be explaining over and over again how I* had *to kill him. I should—"*

"Actually, what you killed wasn't a sentient Other," she said, interrupting my out-loud thoughts. "It was a kelb. A common jinni elemental, often used as a guard dog. Which means—"

"So?" I asked, with perhaps a bit too much venom in my tone for someone who was being let go. "Shouldn't I still be charged with something? Or at least investigated?"

"As much as you would like to be a martyr for Other equal rights by forcing me to arrest you, kelb is a type-C classification Other. It is the Other equivalent of a domestic dog or cat—although who would want something so big and vicious as a pet, I have no idea. We do not file cases against killed pets—especially when it was clearly done in self-defense. That's up to the owner. And since the owner is clearly the killer, I doubt he or she will be filing a suit against you anytime soon."

I took a minute to let that sink in. The creature Egya and I killed was a guard dog of sorts unleashed on us by its master. Not the killer at all.

"Oh?" I said, kind of wishing I'd asked first, ranted later—out-loud thoughts or not. "OK, then." I stood up and put the contents of my purse back into my bag, including my father's mask. Once that was done, I paused and looked Detective Wilcox directly in the eyes. "You said you have footage of the murder."

She nodded.

"So you know who the killer is?"

She gave me a look that said she couldn't answer that.

"Come on—you've got to give me something. The librarian was my friend. The only friend I've made since I got here."

Wilcox shook her head, cursing to herself. "This stays in this room."

"OK—cross my heart." I did so, to show her I was serious.

"The assailant was … blurred."

"Blurred?"

"Yeah—like what you see in documentaries where the interviewee wants to remain anonymous."

"Magic?"

"We can only assume," Detective Wilcox said. "We can gather quite a bit of evidence from the video, but a clear ID? Not as of yet. But we'll get the bastard. I promise you."

"Thank you," I said. Then I pulled my purse strap onto my shoulder and headed out the door.

10

HYENAS AND DENIAL ARE LIKE
OIL AND WATER

*T*he cops were less willing to take me back home than they had been to take me in. I guess it tends to be a one-way flow. Not that it really mattered—the campus was about a twenty-minute walk away. Stepping outside, I saw that dawn had already come and gone, and what greeted me was the morning hustle-bustle of a city getting ready for work.

I wrapped my ruined jacket close to my body, held my purse tight and entered the flow of people walking to work. Montreal is a beautiful city—there's no doubt about it—but at that moment I wanted nothing more than to leave this place far behind. I mean, I had been here less than a day and already I had seen the inside of a police station.

And the inside of my only friend's chest cavity.

But there was one more thing to consider. I had killed. Yes, in self-defense, and it was only an attack dog that I felled. Granted, I killed a fire-breathing attack dog the size of a bull from the jinn's mythical realm of Qa, but still: I killed. Coming to university was my attempt at being a normal, average human. *Normal* and *average* usually means *does not kill* ... but here I was, on day one, stabbing my dirk into some-one's neck. I could chalk it up to seeing my friend strung up like a macabre puppet, something that could believably have brought out my old instincts, but that would be a lie. Truth was, as a vampire, I was *good* at killing. I may have lost most of my powers when I became human, but I didn't lose everything.

What really scared me was how easily it all went down. Once I decided that the creature responsible for killing my friend deserved to die, I acted without hesitation, guilt or remorse. Even now, after the adrenaline had worn out and the heat of the battle had cooled, I felt no regret.

Killing was too easy. At least for me.

I considered my options. I could quit college. After all, I had enough money to last me several lifetimes; given that I was human again, I only needed it to last one. I had an old Victorian mansion waiting for me near Edinburgh's Meadows. And I had enough life experience that the so-called "college experience" wasn't really necessary. When I was considering my options, one of the things the McGill brochure highlighted was how university helped you mature, helped you grow up.

I was over three hundred years old.

Maybe I'd already done all the growing up I needed.

I wasn't sure what to do. Get out of here? Stay? I pulled my purse closer. I could feel the bulge of my father's cherub mask under its plush leather. I thought about my father—the relentless hunter who never quit. What would he think about me leaving? Leaving meant quitting—and I'd never been very good at doing that.

So maybe I don't quit. There were other options. I could leave this university and go somewhere else. *"There are plenty of schools that don't accept Others ... they would be less complicated and—"*

"Coward."

"Excuse me?" I said, turning to see who was calling me names.

I saw Egya sitting under the umbra of a Tim Hortons coffee-shop canopy, where three metal tables and several chairs were positioned. It stank of cigarette smoke and coffee dregs from early commuters. The table he sat at had no ashtray, but it did have two coffees, and from the fact that one of the cups was empty and the other one had a total lack of steam coming out of it, I guessed he had been sitting there for a while.

Which meant he was waiting for me. Great.

He gestured to the seat across from him.

I shook my head. "I don't sit with people who insult me."

"Then don't say things worth insulting."

"Like what?"

"Girl—you talk to yourself. And when you are not talking in a loud voice that birds high in the sky can hear—" He pointed to the sky with long, skinny arms that had firm, defined muscle. He might not have had much meat on him, but there was no doubt he was strong. Also, he was wearing a tight black polo shirt, and I could see his lean muscle bulge from beneath. "—when you are not thinking loudly, you think quietly, mouthing your thoughts so that one with keen eyesight such as myself can read your lips." He caught my eyes with his own emerald eyes, accentuated against his dark skin. "Keen eyes like mine. Please sit—I bought you a coffee."

"Hmph," I said, walking past him.

"I know what you are," he called after me.

I froze, looking around at all the humans walking by.

"And I know what you are pretending to be," he said. "Shall I announce it to the world and free you of your terrible secret? Or will you join—"

"Fine, fine," I huffed, turning around and taking a seat. I grabbed the coffee and downed the now-tepid liquid in one gulp. Given I hadn't eaten in a while, I knew it would only be a matter of minutes before it gave me that anxious coffee buzz. Not that I cared. I wanted to get out of here as quickly as possible, away from this stranger. A finished cup implied a finished conversation. At least, I thought it did. I was still learning human customs. "So," I said, wiping my mouth on a brown paper napkin. "What do you think you know about me?"

"You are no ordinary girl," he said, looking through me just like he had in class.

I shuddered under his gaze. "Well, thank you very much," I said, throwing in as much sarcasm as I could.

"Don't mention it," he replied, either not noticing the scorn in my voice or not caring about it. "It is quite obvious. For one, you fight monsters."

"Not usually. I was in the wrong place at the wrong time and—"

"Most humans simply die when the time and place are wrong. But not you. You fight."

"And what about you? Are you … what, my knight in shining armor?"

He laughed at this, pointing at his orange polo-shirt logo. "I am not a knight, but I do have the horse. But come now," he said, leaning in close, his arms resting on the cool metal of the outdoor table. "Let us address the … what do you Westerners say? … the elephant in the room. A funny expression for a culture that has no indigenous elephants. I, on the other hand, come from a land filled with elephants, and I can say one thing about them—we never take them inside."

"*Très drôle*," I said.

"Most certainly—I am very funny in my native land."

"Ghana?"

"Again, most certainly—but how did you know?"

"I don't think that is how you use 'certainly.'"

He didn't say anything.

"And to answer your question—it's your accent. I spent a lot of time in Africa. All over the world, actually. My father was a—"

"Vampire," he said, more as a statement than anything else.

"Ex- … excuse me?" I picked up my mug to hide behind a sip, forgetting that I'd finished the drink already.

"Or ghoul. But what I know for sure is that you were no shifter."

"Again, excuse me?"

"Shifters are natural liars. You, my dear, cannot lie to save your life, let alone hide your past. And given that vampires, ghouls and zombies were the only other creatures to become human once more when the gods left …"

"And you know all this from what? Experience?"

"Most certainly."

I grimaced at the expression. "Just because you were a … a what?"

"Were-hyena."

"Don't you mean were*wolf*?"

"I would if that was what I changed into, but wolves are not indigenous to my homeland. Hyenas, on the other hand—"

"And because you were a monster, once upon a time, you … what? Think I was, too? And a ghoul, at that?"

He sipped his drink, smirking. "Possibly."

"But ghouls," I said, looking for a cop-out, "aren't they … ghoulish?"

"Not all of them. In my homeland, there were many types of ghouls, some of whom could lure their prey with promises of pleasure, both divine and carnal, and—"

"I am *not* a ghoul."

"*Was*, not *am*. I am speaking of your past."

"OK—then read my lips. I—was not—am not—nor will I ever be—a ghoul."

"Then vampire."

"I am *not*—"

"Again—not *am*. Before."

"My past? My past! That is exactly what I don't want to speak about with anyone, let alone someone like you." I stood up in frustration. "Am, was, will be—I'm not a GoneGodDamn—" I caught myself before I shouted, and leaned in close "—vampire."

Egya gave me a smug look. "Liar."

"Asshole."

"Most certainly," he said with a wicked smile.

* * *

I left Egya in the wake of my rage.

GoneGodDamn it, damn it, damn it!

My anger affirmed his suspicions, I was sure, but I couldn't help it. His accusations just confirmed what I was afraid of: *I can't be in a place where people know who or what I am. I came here to have a new start. To forget my past. Fresh future.* Egya might tell people who I was. Or worse, they might make me sign up with the damn government Other registration.

Damn it!

I may have been conflicted about quitting before, but now that I had someone like Egya on my tail, I just might have to leave. New start, new place ... without that were-dog chasing me.

"I'm going to have to quit university, aren't I?" I groaned. "Well, at least I made it to the dawn of my second day. That's practically a record."

END OF PART 2

PART III
INTERMISSION

"Joseph Campbell, in *The Hero of a Thousand Faces*, outlines the commonalities shared by all religions.

"Origin stories: Christians, the Jewish faith and Muslims all have the Garden of Eden; the Hopi have the Four Worlds; Shinto has the Tenchikaibyaku.

"Then, of course, there is the flood story: the Abrahamic religions have Noah's flood; the Norse have Bergelmir's escape; the Sumerians have the Gilgamesh flood myth.

"The parallels go on and on. Forbidden knowledge, trickster beings, concepts of an afterlife and so on ... But there is one less-known, less-discussed commonality that we see in almost every religion—especially when we look at their early practices. Can anyone tell me what that is?

"What? No takers?

"Very well then. Let me tell you. Sacrifice. Almost every recorded religion is known to have some form of human sacrifice as part of its canon. Even Judaism and Christianity speak of animal sacrifice in the books of Exodus, Leviticus and Numbers, to name a few. The methods of sacrifice might be different, but the purpose is universal.

"To please the gods.

"Well, we've all seen how that's worked out, haven't we?"

11

ACTIVISTS PLAY FOOTBALL, TOO

*D*ay Two of me trying to be human and already I felt like crap.

It wasn't even 10:00 a.m.!

I wanted to go back to the dorms and curl up under my duvet—if I had a duvet left. For all I knew, Deirdre, that socially unversed changeling roommate of mine, might have taken out all those goose feathers to make wings for herself.

Whoever said your time in university would be the best days of your life clearly didn't have mine in mind.

As I walked past the Eaton Centre and toward the main gate, I passed by McGill's statue and paused to look at the dark copper man. He held on to his hat against an endless wind as he pointed toward … what? … the future? The next steps in evolution?

I followed his finger and saw that he was pointing toward the Montreal train station. Maybe he was telling me to get out. Was this a sign?

Whatever! Sign or not, I wouldn't be here for long. It was time for this girl to exit stage right and … and … do something else. What, I had no idea, but I'd figure it out. Determined that leaving was my best choice, I turned on my heels and headed to campus. The way I figured it, I'd wrap up some loose ends, inform Student Admin that I was dropping out and pack up my dorm. If I hurried, I could get it all done by the weekend.

As I walked to campus, I was so deep in figuring out exactly how one drops out of university that I walked right into Justin—for the second day in a row.

"Whoa," he said. "Seems the only way to get your attention is by getting in your way."

I looked up to see him smiling at me with his kind yet powerful jaw, the sun shining off his perfect black locks ... and what's more, he was holding me, two gentle hands cradling my elbows. All we needed was for him to be shirtless and me in some loosely draped corset and we could be the cover of a Harlequin romance novel.

"Ahh, sorry," I said, making sure to not pull away. "I've got a lot on my mind."

He didn't let go. "Yeah, well, welcome to university. A lot can happen."

"Oh my," I thought, *"It's been a long time since I've been in a man's arms and not wanted to rip out his throat."*

"Excuse me?" he said. From his confusion, I gathered he didn't quite make out what I'd said. Thank the GoneGods—that must have been my "quiet" thinking, as Egya had called it.

"Nothing," I said, swooning. "I was just saying—a lot on my mind."

"No kidding," he said. "I've been looking all over campus for you. Even went to your dorm room, but your roommate said you hadn't been home all night." He hesitated.

"What is it?" I asked.

"You know what happened, right? Last night?"

I nodded.

"Rumors are that you were there."

I pursed my lips and looked down, as if in thought. After what felt like an eternity, where I debated between telling Justin everything or denying it all, I eventually settled on a harmless nod. There was no point in hiding it—everyone would find out eventually. If, that was, Egya hadn't already distributed flyers.

"Wow," Justin said, lifting one of his hands so he could nervously run his fingers through his perfect hair. "Did you see what happened?"

"No," I said. "I got there too late. The killer was still there—"

"Did you see who it was?"

I shook my head. "No. Whoever it was escaped before I could get a look at him ... or her. Then before I could get a good look around, the killer's jinni guard dog attacked me."

"Jinni *what*?"

"Jinni guard dog—think normal guard dog, only about twelve times bigger, with a long, spiky tail and lava for blood."

"And what, it attacked you?"

"Yep, but I managed to ..." I paused.

"To ...?" Justin's eyes widened as he waited for my answer.

Again I thought about lying—but the truth would come out sooner or later. *It always does,* I lamented. I looked away. I didn't want to see Justin's reaction when I told him.

"... to kill it."

"What? How?"

"An old dagger that fell out of one of the display cases. I stabbed the thing—jinni or not, it wasn't immune to being stabbed."

"How in the ...?" he started, but trailed off.

I knew he must have been judging me for what I did; he was probably thinking of an excuse to get away from me. Hell, he was probably afraid to leave too quickly, lest I stab him, too, and—

Then I felt a finger on my chin, gently guiding my face up. I let it, and a second later I was looking into his deep blue, endless, concerned eyes.

"You must have been terrified," he said.

I nodded.

"What did the police say?"

"That it was a Class C Other. Seems it's not a crime to kill a Class C—so if you see any around ..." I made a slitting-throat gesture that was meant to be a joke.

Justin did not laugh.

Great.

Hoping to leave my poor-taste joke behind me, I quickly added, "But given how it almost ate me, I think it's more of an attack dog with Terminator-like dedication."

"Ah-hah," he nervously laughed. "And what about the killer? I'm guessing anyone with that kind of creature following them around for protection is an Other of a … different … classification?"

I stopped for a second and thought about the implication of his question. "The killer is an *Other*!"

"Um," Justin said, "isn't that obvious?"

"Not really. But if it *is* an Other, its classification would be telling. The police can use that as a clue."

Justin nodded, but then the implication of my words hit me like a bag of bricks.

"The police *will* use that. They'll single out Others. That's what you mean." I looked up accusingly. "In other words, the killer is someone who is easily identifiable by the shape of their body, color of their skin or the extra appendages on their body."

"I didn't mean it like that," he said, drawing away. "I mean it like you said … it's a clue. A narrowing down of suspects or something."

Fine—I gave him a pass, but only because he was so gorgeous. And he did seem sincere. "That's what the cops think."

"And you?"

I nodded begrudgingly. "I can't think of many humans who can summon a jinni, can you?"

"No," he chuckled, "I can't."

"But still," I said, "don't tell anyone that the killer is probably an Other. They're already being picked on, and it took so much work for a university to open its doors to Others. The last thing I want to do is add fuel to the already fear-filled fire."

He winced at this.

"What?" I asked.

"It might be too late for that," he said, handing me a red flyer.

I took the flyer and read it:

OTHER KILLER ON CAMPUS!
BEWARE, BE VIGILANT AND BE SURE TO CALL SECURITY
IF YOU SEE ANY SUSPICIOUS OTHERS ABOUT.

The flyer featured a picture of an ogre lurking about, but the funny thing about the image was that it was taken from the *World of Warcraft* movie. *"Real ogres don't look like that. For one thing, their skin is more of an avocado green, and it's covered in a lot more hair and—"*

"You know a lot about Others," Justin said.

"Too much," I groaned. "I am—was—thinking about majoring in Other Studies. Hence why I was at the library."

"Was majoring?"

"Am … might … Haven't decided," I lied. The appropriate helping verb was more like *won't* … as in *won't be studying anything anymore.* I handed him back the flyer. "This is bad. Any Other student is a target now. Even your dorm buddy, Sal."

"I know," he said solemnly. "That's why I'm going to give a speech at the candlelight vigil tonight."

"Vigil?"

"Yeah, we're holding a memorial. I'm going to give a speech and invite everyone to our O^3 party."

"What? You're using this as a way to promote your party?"

"No, no," he said, his cheeks flushing. "I didn't mean it like that. The whole point of the party is to start the school year in an all-inclusive, everyone-is-welcome sort of way. Others included, of all body shapes, skin colors and extra appendages." That made me smile, which gave him confidence. "I figured if we can get everyone to party together—you know, they'll all get along."

"Make love, not war," I said.

He laughed at this, not knowing that I wasn't trying to be funny or cute. I had attended the Mother's Day Peace March in 1965 (well, attended the after-dusk part, at least). Nowadays, it was a cliché printed on a T-shirt. But back then, it meant something.

I looked up at Justin. "I guess I see what you're trying to do," I said.

"Look, I know it's not enough, but it's something. It will make sense tonight, I promise. Will you come?"

"To the party?"

"No—the vigil. For my speech. I'm super-nervous ... I could use a friendly face."

I didn't say anything.

Justin gave me an empathetic smile and said, "I know you've been through a lot, Kat. Think about it. I could use all the support I can get."

"What about your dorm buddies?"

"They'll be there. The humans, at least. We're encouraging Sal to lay low for a while."

"OK." I nodded. "I'll think about it."

"Good." Then, looking at his wristwatch, he said, "I'm late for class. Maybe see you tonight, but definitely see you at the O^3 party?"

The O^3 party was this weekend, which meant delaying leaving by a day or two. I could go and pretend it was my goodbye party—even if no one attending knew me, knew I was leaving or cared. Still, I should at least attend one college party to see if they lived up to all the hype 1980s comedies promised.

I nodded at Justin.

"Great," he said, flashing a big, perfect smile as he started to jog away. "Glad I can make you commit to at least one of them."

And with that, he was gone, leaving me at the entrance of campus, holding the Other-hating flyer. I crumpled it up and tossed it in the nearest rubbish bin.

Arrgh—Others! I wondered if the gods knew how many problems sending them to Earth would cause. If they would have still done it.

My guess was ... yes.

I guess "hindsight is 20/20" only applies if you actually *care* about the people you've left behind.

12
WISE SAGES AND PALE WHITE RIDERS

*S*o I was stuck here until after the weekend. Fine. Just meant more time to get my affairs in order. Affairs—hah! All those college movies talked about hooking up with boys, falling in love, dancing, partying ... living. Sure, I saw students playing frisbee, hanging out by the founder statue and generally just chilling on campus, but what I didn't see was me being a part of that.

Maybe I don't deserve it.

"Oh, shush," I growled at myself. I deserve to live and be happy just like everyone else.

Pulling my purse closer, I walked into the Admin building and straight to a receptionist with hipster glasses and purple hair tied into a ponytail.

"I want to drop out," I said.

She looked at me over the rims of her glasses. "Day Two jitters?" she asked.

"Day Two coming-to-my-senses," I said.

"Uh-huh. Student ID, please."

I opened my purse and handed the laminated ID card to her.

She keyed my details into her computer. "A student advisor will see you shortly. Until then, have a seat."

* * *

I went into the waiting room, where three humans huddled at one end and four Others hung out on the other side. The awkwardness between the two groups was palpable. The Others were comprised of two cherubs, an oni demon and a gargoyle that looked like a stone dragon the size of a tomcat. Among the humans was the mousey girl from Gardner Hall (the one who'd handed Deirdre some soil) and a guy who looked like he was auditioning for *Small Town Hick* at the local school theater.

I nodded at Mousey Girl, giving her a knowing smile. She promptly looked away in fear, blushing as she pushed up her thick-framed glasses.

The two cherubs were both only five inches tall; one looked like a baby with a halo and dove-like wings, while the other one resembled a cute, miniature devil with bat wings. I figured them for shoulder cherubs. You know—the angels who sat on your shoulder and encourage you to do good or bad. Given how they huddled together, I knew they were scared. Made sense ... shoulder cherubs were meant to sit invisibly on your shoulders and guide you through the murky waters of morality. They weren't used to being visible, shoulderless and sitting in a human waiting room.

They were harmless.

The oni demon, on the other hand, looked like the manga version of the classic Western image of the Devil—red skin, pointy tail, horns —but with huge eyes and tusks that protruded up out of his lower jaw. He was clearly nervous as well, grinding his teeth together, which, because of the large metal ring in one of his tusks, made a clicking sound every time he separated his jaw.

With each of the demon's tusk-grinding clicks, Hick Boy clenched his fists like he was just itching to charge at the oni. *"Stupid human— you'll need a crowbar or machete to do any damage against that thing. Its skin is tougher than a coconut shell. Believe me—I once got into a fight with one of them on Zamami Island off of Okinawa's mainland when—"*

Everyone was looking at me. *OK, girl,* I thought—in my head this time—*go with it*. I turned to Hick Boy and said, "You're clearly scared of this guy, otherwise you wouldn't be acting so aggro."

"You mind your own business," Hick Boy said, in a Southern accent I couldn't quite place. Mississippi? Possibly Georgia.

How cliché, I thought before saying, "I can't mind my business when I see you trying to burn holes in that poor guy. Can't you see, he's just as scared as you are?"

"*Kowai janai,*" the oni demon boomed, at which Hick Boy stood up. So did the demon, while Mousey Girl screamed.

I got between human and demon, all of my five-foot-nothing frame separating the two massive bodies of aggro testosterone, and yelled, "Yes, you *are* scared. Both of you are."

I must have said it with a force that belied my size, because both of them stopped.

Pointing at the oni demon, I said, "Do you speak English?"

The oni demon nodded, his tusk ring clicking.

"OK," I said. "The rest of us would be more comfortable if you don't yell—and if you need to yell at all, do it in English so that everyone who can't speak Japanese can understand you."

Hick Boy chuckled at this.

"And you," I growled, pointing up at him. "I thought you Southerners were all about hospitality and being good ol' Christians or whatever. Where are those Southern sensibilities your mama taught you? Huh?"

"My hospitality doesn't extend to freaks," he said.

"Bold words for a guy in flannel. It's summer and not 1976."

I saw Mousey Girl's eyes widen with terror. I needed to calm the situation down if I didn't want to get into yet a third fight in two days, and my sassy comebacks weren't helping. I made a soothing gesture and said, "I have an idea—if everyone will sit down, I think I can fix this."

Hick Boy and oni demon stared down at me for a long moment before finally sitting down in agreement.

"Good," I said. "Presumably you all are here to drop out."

Several nods greeted me, with Hick Boy adding, "I didn't sign up to go to school with a bunch of freaks."

"I'll get to you in a minute," I said, glaring. "First, you." I pointed at Mousey Girl. "You're scared, right?"

She nodded.

"I've seen you around. You live in the dorms? Gardner Hall?"

"No, I live off campus. I came up to visit a friend, but—"

"You saw lots of weird creatures about, so you just went home where it's safe?"

Again she nodded.

"So might I offer you an alternative? See that guy over there?" I gestured at the stone gargoyle. "He's a protector. And given that he's here, willing to leave this place, I'm willing to bet he has no one to protect. *Do* you?"

The gargoyle closed its stone eyes in despondence. It let out a long sigh that sounded like pepper being ground, then shook its head. I bent down close and tentatively put out my arm, as I'd read these little protectors preferred. Seeing my arm before it, the gargoyle's eyes widened in awe. Without further hesitation, it leapt from the chair to my arm, its stone claws gripping my jacket sleeve. Ah, well—the jacket was ruined anyway. That grinding-pepper noise picked back up, but it wasn't sighing. Was that … was it purring? It seemed to like me. Up close, I saw that the gargoyle had several runes carved along its body —beautiful, really.

I walked over to where Mousey Girl sat, scowling at how she cowered in her seat as the gargoyle on my arm got closer. "Problem," I pointed at Mousey Girl, then gestured to the gargoyle. "Meet Solution." She still seemed nervous that the stone creature was so close, so I added, "Why don't you two just go for a walk together? Out in public, with lots of eyes watching you. The campus is a safe place to get to know each other. And if it works out … well, this could be a win-win."

Mousey Girl considered this before finally nodding and standing up. The gargoyle jumped off my arm and the two of them left together.

"Freaks," Hick Boy snorted.

I turned to glare at him again, but what had just occurred had given me a change of heart. Instead I sighed.

"No, not freaks. Just different. You say your Southern sensibilities don't extend to them. But is that the right thing to do? I mean, deep down?"

I walked over to the shoulder cherubs and, extending my hands, invited them to jump on. I carried them over to Hick Boy. He tried to move away, but before he could, I said, "What? Scared of something smaller than a ferret?"

He shook his head defiantly and took a deep breath. "I don't know what you are trying to do, but—"

"Shh ... just listen."

The angels began talking in his ears and—miraculously, in a world where miracles had left with the gods—Hick Boy listened. The thing about shoulder cherubs is they don't tell you what's right and what's wrong; they don't even tell you *you're* right or wrong. They tell you *your* right and wrong. Everyone has a different moral compass. Well, not *everyone* ... and some of those who *do* have one clearly need to get it recalibrated ...

Sorry. I've clearly let my analogy run away from me.

The point is, shoulder cherubs ... the words they whisper into your ears are *guided* by that moral compass. And whatever they were saying to Hick Boy, it worked. His shoulders relaxed, his fists unclenched and he actually smiled—not the prettiest thing, but definitely an improvement for him.

I pointed to the oni demon. "Now, you. What's your name?"

"Takashi."

"Good. Now, Takashi, loosen that ring in your tusk and ... smile."

The oni demon pulled out the tusk ring and tried to smile, which, judging by how big those tusks were, was not an easy task, and did not yield the most aesthetically pleasing results. It was awkward, not very human-like, but somehow endearing.

"Now, might I suggest one more thing?" I said to the two monstrous smiling buffoons. "Oni demons, among other things, are famous for distilling their own sake." Takashi nodded proudly. "And Southerners are famous for their bourbon. Why not have a drink together first, kill each other later? Or at least talk it out. Can you do that?"

"*Hai.*" Takashi bowed his head, then, correcting himself, said, "Yes."

The good angel whispered in Hick Boy's ear, but he didn't move. Then the devil said something, and Hick Boy's smile turned unquestionably wicked. "Don't mind if I do."

The two of them left at that—although that wicked smile of Hick Boy's was a bit worrisome. Ah, well. God didn't create the world in a day.

Phew, I thought, sitting down in a now-empty room. *That went better than expected.* Satisfied with my little display, I picked up a magazine, but before I could settle I heard, "Katrina Darling? Given that you just cleared the room, I guess you're next."

I looked up, expecting to see a human counselor, but what—or rather, *who*—greeted me was Medusa.

As in the one-of-a-kind, Queen-of-the-friggin'-Gorgons *Medusa.*

"Ahh, hi," I said, gulping, trying not to stare at her snakes. "It's a pleasure to meet you. I'm a huge fan."

13

SNAKES AND SAGES

*L*iving for over three hundred years gives you a lot of time to see just about everything you want to see. But while Medusa was one of my idols, she'd only become *see*able in the last four years, and I hadn't yet had the pleasure.

And believe me, the pleasure was all mine.

She was beautiful—creamy skin, flawless symmetry, everything you'd expect from a Greek goddess, all topped with the more-than-intimidating nest of vipers cascading around her head, surprisingly similar to a regular hairstyle. But what surprised me was her age. Sure, I was living proof that someone could live an incredibly long life yet still resemble a teenager, but I would never have guessed that my idol—Medusa, Queen of the Gorgons—and I would actually have something in common! As I followed her out of the waiting room, I noticed every fashionable article of clothing on her body with delight.

We have the same fashion sense! Medusa's stylish, just like me!

Oh, GoneGods, I was fangirling so hard. I had heard she was on campus, but I never expected to meet her face to face … this was the best day ever. Then I remembered why I was here and what had happened in the last twenty-four hours and, well, my joy came crashing down like a flaming Zeppelin.

Medusa led me into a tiny room just big enough for a small desk and two chairs. In an effort to maximize space, shelves had been fashioned to the wall behind her and climbed all the way up to the ceiling. They housed all sorts of files and books, and one of them even had Medusa's purse and several of her personal effects out, like a cubby or an open-ended locker.

An old PC sat on the desk. She gestured to one seat and, taking the other, began tapping away at her keyboard. Two of her snakes rose high about her head and, using their mouths, picked up a bowl of jellybeans from one of the shelves. They placed the bowl in front of me.

"Help yourself," Medusa said, not looking up from the PC screen.

The two snakes flicked their tongues at me. *Snake hospitality?*

"Johnny and Alfie are two of my nicer snakes," Medusa said, punching 'Enter' twice on her computer keyboard. " 'Katrina Darling —Major Undeclared. Gardner resident.' Interesting—says here that under 'Roommate Preference,' you ticked *None*. An Other roommate?"

"Changeling."

She looked away from the screen. "Yikes—they're ..."

"Monumental tree huggers?"

"Quite literally, in my experience," Medusa said. She gave me an appraising look, not unkindly. "But something tells me you can handle it. After all, you were quite resourceful in the way you handled the tension in the waiting room."

"Thanks."

"That said, I'm not sure how I feel about encouraging students to start drinking at—" she looked at her watch "—ten-thirty in the morning."

"Yeah, well ..." I blushed. "College life," I added lamely.

"So you want to drop out?"

"I just don't know if this place is for me. I mean—if my first day is any indication, then I definitely don't belong here."

"So drop out," Medusa said without any hint of sarcasm or irony. "I did."

"Excuse me? I heard ... I mean, aren't *you* a student here?"

"Was. They opened up the school for Others last semester and I was the first to enroll. For my one and only semester here I studied Sociology—which is really just a funny way to say 'Studying Humans.' I even got a 3.96 GPA. I had a full scholarship—which, given that I donated the Golden Fleece to Other Studies, they kind of owed me. Loved it here."

"And you dropped out?"

"Yeah."

"Why?"

The largest snake on her head dipped into her purse and pulled out a badge. "Thanks, Marty," she said, handing it over to me.

Looking at the badge, I said, "You're a Paradise Lot Police Officer?"

"Not yet, but if everything goes right, I will be in two years."

"So what are you doing here? Isn't Paradise Lot ..." I thought about it. "Where *is* Paradise Lot?"

"Oh, you know the place," she said. "That island in New England's Lake District. The new home for most Other refugees. I'm not there now because the school asked me and a couple other Others to come to campus at the start of the semester to do a few guest lectures on human, Other relations. You know, talk to humans who want to drop out because of Other attendance. They figured a familiar head of snakes such as myself—" the snakes all hissed, as if saying "Ta-daaaaaa!" "—would help with the adjustment ... so, surprise, here I am."

"And you're handling my case because ..."

"Because," she said drawing out the word just like I did, "I was visiting the Head of Student Admin when some five-foot nothing, cute girl came in and did what you did. Well, I was so impressed that I asked if I could handle your case and well ... here we are."

"You think I'm cute?" I blurted and immediately regretted it. As my cheeks cycled through seventy shades of red, I tried to recover from my little faux pas by asking, "And Paradise Lot Police—what's that about?"

Medusa smirked before saying, "I took a look around me and asked myself, 'Where can I do the most good?' My choices were to stay here, study humans, then get a job with some political party or activist group ... or I could go to Paradise Lot and help out my own kind there."

"So you chose to become a cop?"

"Paradise Lot is quickly becoming the only Other-majority city in the world. You know what that means?"

"That Others enjoy a good wordplay on classic literature?"

She shook her head. "There are so many kinds of Others from different traditions, religions and folklore that the mishmash of cultures in such a small place will mean a lot of conflicts. And right now, because Others are the newcomers, we need to prove that we can not only live on Earth but that we will be productive, peaceful citizens. If the world turns on their TV and sees fighting in Paradise Lot, their distrust of Others will only grow. I went there to play my part in keeping the peace.

"But that doesn't mean I can't come up here to show humans like you that we Others aren't to be feared. After all, if the big, bad, turn-you-to-stone Medusa is a nice gal, then maybe, just maybe, the other Others are nice, too. Right?"

"Yeah ... I have to say you are not what I expected."

She leaned forward and put a hand on my arm. Several of her snakes, including the big green viper that came out of the crown of her head, winked at me. "Girlfriend—we never are," she said with a smirk.

I chuckled.

"You have a nice laugh—and a kind smile," Medusa said. "You're tough, smart—a great sense of style." She looked down at my outfit appreciatively, and I enforced every ounce of my willpower to not let out a high-pitched fangirl squeak. "A girl like you should not only fit right in, you should be the belle of the ball."

"You'd think. I mean, if you watch all those college movies ... *Animal House, Revenge of the Nerds, Van Wilder*—"

"*Legally Blonde*," we said in unison.

"Yeah," I said, laughing. "Exactly. I mean—look at me. I'm basically Reese Witherspoon without the annoying voice."

"So what's the trouble?"

"Last night, it was … it was terrible."

"Yes, you've mentioned. What happened that was so bad?"

I shook my head. I didn't want to rehash the previous night's events. It did surprise me that Medusa hadn't heard about it yet—she wanted to be a police officer, didn't she?—but I would have felt this way regardless of what had happened. If I were to be totally honest with myself, I had already been feeling uneasy before all the stuff at the library. "It doesn't matter," I finally said. "Let's just say it's painfully evident that I don't fit in here."

"Just because you had a bad day doesn't mean you're going to have a bad year. A day is a day. And in my experience, what happens today doesn't predict what will happen tomorrow."

"I think it does. If anything, it predicted that I'm not like everyone else."

"And that's a bad thing?" Medusa said, petting her lead snake. "If I was like everyone else, I wouldn't have Marty here keeping me company."

"Yeah—but you're *Medusa*. You are literally a legend! I'm just—"

"A Darling."

"Excuse me?"

"You are Katrina Darling—*that's* somebody."

"Yeah, but—"

"So drop out," she repeated.

I looked up at her, once more surprised. Wasn't she supposed to be trying to convince me to stay?

My shocked look was met with a kind, warm smile of understanding. "Or stay—it doesn't matter to me. But whatever you do, do so because it is where you can do the most good."

"That's just the thing. I don't know if me staying will lead to any good."

"Do you think you can do more good somewhere else? That's why I left."

I didn't say anything.

Medusa's snakes hissed impatiently, and the former Queen of the

Gorgons closed my file. "For what it's worth, I think you should stay. The way you helped the students in the waiting room proves you have a knack for bridging the divide between our species. McGill could use more students like you."

I shook my head hesitantly. "I don't know …"

"And you don't *need* to know. Not right now. Just think about it. Get through the weekend. From what I hear, McConnell Hall is having a big party tomorrow."

I smiled. She hears about parties but not on-campus murders. She'd have a rude awakening at police orientation. "Yeah—the O^3 costume ball. 'Ringing in the Apocalypse.'"

"The apocalypse already happened, and we're still here."

"I know," I said. "If I had been on the planning committee, I would have suggested the party be called 'The World Without End' or something like that."

Medusa tilted her head, nodding in approval. More than approval —like she was proud of me or something. It felt nice to have someone so warm and inviting look at me like that, especially my literal hero.

"Yeah," Medusa said. "Like I said—I like your style. The weekend … OK? If it doesn't go well, then you can come back here and drop out. Deal?"

I didn't move.

"Deal?" she repeated with more force in her voice. I was painfully aware of every snake on her head staring at me intently, like they were trying to turn me to stone.

I nodded. Reluctantly. "Yeah, sure. Will … will you be here?"

"Sadly, no—I'm back to Paradise Lot later today. But someone else will be here, and I'll be sure to put in your file that you are a special case. A very special case, indeed," she said gesturing for the door. "And in answer to your early question … as a button," she added as I stood.

"Excuse me?"

"Yes, I think you're cute. As a button." Then she—and all of her snakes—simultaneously winked at me.

14

THE TRUTH, THE WHOLE TRUTH, AND NOTHING BUT THE TRUTH

The Truth, the Whole Truth, and Nothing but the Truth (... So Help Me, GoneGods)

I left Student Admin feeling more confused than ever. TV dads (my primary source of fatherly advice, given that I ate mine a few centuries back) always say their daughters don't have enough life experience to make the right decisions. They imply that life experience comes from age, from doing and seeing things. From living. I'd been alive for over three hundred years and I still didn't feel I had enough life experience to decide anything.

My stomach grumbled. Seeing that it was almost noon, I walked down into off-campus housing (affectionately known as the Student Ghetto) to find something to eat and—lo and behold—what was the first place I stumbled upon? A döner kebab shop opening up.

Two birds, one kebab, I thought as I walked in, thanking the Gone-Gods for small miracles.

* * *

"I know what you are," I said. "You are Mergen—or, rather, Mergen's avatar."

I found Mergen sitting in an alleyway behind the Religious Studies Library (a building that was adjacent, but oddly unconnected to, the Other Studies Library).

At my words, a weak smile appeared on Mergen's face—and I knew I was right. Or the Old Librarian had been right. He was Mergen. *Score one for you, librarian. Your last point before the buzzer,* I thought with a heavy heart. Mergen's eyes brightened and there was a glint of hope in them. I guess that's what happens when someone acknowledges your existence, and I suspected that in the four years he'd been mortal, I was the first person who had actually called him by his name.

The avatar was sitting on the ground, looking weaker and more emaciated than ever. His skin was also whiter. No, that wasn't it exactly—it was more … transparent. Like he was literally fading away into nothing.

"I don't know much about you yet, except to say you represent Truth and Wisdom—that, and you're Turkish. Which is why I got you this." I handed him the döner kebab, and he took it with a hand so absent of flesh that bone poked from his fingertips.

Picking the cleanest plot of ground near him, I sat down and unwrapped the falafel I'd bought for myself. Glancing over at the avatar dude, I noticed his expression had changed drastically. Whereas initially he had looked grateful and slightly better, now he sat staring down at the sandwich, his head hung low in despair once more.

"Oh, come on!" I said. "This is from your homeland. Are you really telling me a Turkish deity doesn't eat döner kebabs?"

He shook his head and uttered, "The truth?" It sounded like a question.

"Yes, the truth," I said. "What *do* you eat? A friend of mine debated this very topic with me before— Well, he's gone now."

The avatar pursed his lips, not answering, his impossibly white skin shining in the sunlight.

"Are you a vegetarian?" I asked, taking the kebab and handing him my falafel. "I am, too. At least, I am now."

He took the sandwich, which was essentially mashed deep-fried chickpeas, and sniffed it. Then he groaned.

"Look, no judgment here. If you tell me you eat kittens, I'll help you find a kitten. I won't watch you eat, but I won't judge you either," I lied. Well, maybe not *lied*. I exaggerated. I *would* judge him. But my judgment would fall short of condemnation. After all, I'd eaten a lot worse than kittens.

A *lot* worse.

But he just shook his head.

"OK," I said, sliding next to him. "If you can't eat that, can I?"

He handed me back the falafel.

I ripped away the foil and took a bite. I felt guilty eating in front of him, but it was a necessary part of my plan. I wanted to get this guy so hungry and frustrated, eventually he'd break and tell me what he ate that was so disgusting he just didn't want to share with me.

"You know," I said, taking another bite and speaking to him around it, trying to show him just how delicious it was, "I'm not sure I'm cut out for this place."

He nodded. I couldn't tell if he was agreeing with me or simply acknowledging my feelings.

"When I first came here, I thought: here's a place where I can have a second chance. A place where no one knows me, knows what I've done, where I've been. A fresh start. A chance to become brand-new."

I heard Mergen smack his lips—presumably the Turkish godly equivalent of *I hear you, girl!*

"But then I got here ... and you know what I discovered? That you may be done with the past, but the past isn't necessarily done with you. So much for a fresh, brand-new start, right?"

Mergen groaned again. And not in the *I'm in pain* kind of way. More like *This feels so good, it's bordering on creepy.* A little nervous that Mergen was perving out on me, I turned to see what was making him so happy. He was looking right at me, the corners of his lips turned slightly upward in an expression that simultaneously had a grateful and *Don't stop* quality to it. But it wasn't his expression that most astonished me—it was the transformation he had just gone through. The avatar was still pale, but he wasn't as transparent as before. And what's more, his hands had some meat to them. They almost looked normal.

"What's … going on?" I asked, amazed that anyone or anything could change so much in so little time with no nourishment in between.

"The truth," he muttered.

"The truth? What are you talking about?"

Then it hit me—when I had asked him what he ate, he'd said, "The truth." Because of the way he inflected the end of the word, I had interpreted it as a question—as in, "Do you want the truth about what I eat?" And when he didn't answer that question, I thought it was because he didn't want to tell me. But seeing how his skin fleshed out and how he perked up a bit when I told him about my own inner struggles, I realized that when I asked him what he ate and he said, "The truth," he was telling me the truth.

This guy doesn't eat chicken or beef, lamb kebabs or broccoli. He eats Truth, with a capital *T*, the honest-to-the-GoneGods *Truth*. And me admitting what I did, me telling him how I truly felt, that fed him. "Holy crow … you eat the Truth?"

He nodded.

"And I guess with everything going on around here, the Truth isn't in high supply, huh? People are mulling about, denying how they're fed up with the world, not really confronting what is really going on, right?"

Again he nodded, but I also noted that his skin, although still impossibly white, was gaining a little bit more meat on it.

"OK," I said. "If I tell you some of my own Truth, will you keep it secret?"

"To my grave," he said softly.

I believed him. After all, a creature who ate truth probably couldn't lie. That would be akin to poisoning himself.

I took a deep breath. "I used to be a vampire. And I haven't told anyone, because I'm ashamed of who I was and what I did."

His eyes turned down and he grabbed his stomach, as if he had a bellyache.

"What's wrong?" I asked. "I didn't lie to you—it's the truth."

"It is ... *half* the truth," he said.

"Half the truth? What more do you want from me?"

"All of it."

I started feeling a bit defensive. "I *gave* you all of it."

"No ... no, you didn't."

"What do you mean?" I could feel my frustration rising in me. What did this guy want? For me to bare my soul just because he was hungry? He would have to take the truth I gave him.

He gave me a knowing look. "Thank you," he said.

"For what?"

"For trying."

That really boiled my blood. Trying? *Trying!* I just told him my biggest, darkest secret—and it wasn't *enough*? I grabbed my purse and stood up in a huff. "You know, I understand that you eat the Truth and all, but you're still a beggar. And beggars—they can't be choosers. You should be grateful for what you can get!"

At this, his eyes widened and a satisfied smile painted his face. "Mmmm," he moaned. "That is true. And tasty."

I stared at him. "You're weird."

"Yes," he agreed, rubbing his belly.

"And you creep me out."

"I do, don't I?" he said, smacking his lips.

"And I am leaving," I said, turning on my heel.

"Yes ... that is the Truth, and it is delicious!"

Oh, brother ... I'd met a lot of Others in my life, but this Mergen guy took the prize.

15

JESSICA FLETCHER, YOU ARE NOT DARLING

J walked up the hill in a huff, stomping my feet down with an unnecessary intensity as I made my way back to Gardner Hall. *"The truth? The TRUTH?!"* I thought (probably out loud, if we're being truthful). *"He wants the Truth?! Well, maybe the Truth is that a creature like him is too weak to live in the GoneGod World. Maybe he needs to get off his high horse and eat some humble pie like the rest of us. Maybe he should burn all the magic time he has left to blow smoke up his own a—"*

A couple of students who were meandering down the hill looked at me as I passed by them. Not that I cared. I was too busy dealing with the "Truth"! Frustrated and dejected, I entered through the building's front door and made my way to the basement stairs. All I wanted was my bed, my iPad and a movie. Preferably a slasher.

And I was so close to getting just that.

I was only a few yards away when I heard the unmistakable voice of my changeling roommate in the laundry room. *"Never, you foul, disrespectful urchin!"* I heard Deirdre cry out.

"What did you call me?" I heard another voice say, more in confusion than actual anger. "Look, I don't know what your problem is, but that's *mine*. I'm the one that picked it up. I get to keep it."

"For what purpose? To display on your mantel? You did not dispatch the creature—you have no claims to keep a part of him as a trophy. This being—this piece of 'stone,' as you call it—deserves a proper burial. An appropriate farewell."

"Leave him alone," I heard another, higher-pitched voice say.

"It's just a piece of stone."

"Stone? Stone!" Deirdre's rage was intensifying. I didn't know the changeling well enough to know if she could control her temper or not, and my fear was that if she did lose it and attack this guy, she'd rip him to shreds. Literally. Changelings don't mess around. Given all the resurrection magic that used to exist among the UnSeelie Court, they tended to destroy their victims' bodies to the point of no return.

I stepped inside the laundry room—a bleak space painted orange and holding six machines. Two of them were running, their tumblers reverberating white noise as the smell of detergent and fabric softener wafted through the room. Inside, there was some kid with an Iron Man hoodie, holding his hands up as if in surrender. A classically pretty, tall blonde stood next to him in what looked like her pajamas, holding an empty white basket.

Uh-oh. She looked like she was getting ready to scream.

The kid in the hoodie took a step back and diverted his gaze. Big mistake. He had just showed Deirdre that he was scared. As a fae warrior, her instincts would be to press her advantage—any true warrior would feel the same way. Destroy your enemy however you can. And if they're weak? Just means an easier victory for you.

Deirdre pulled back her fist and took a step into him. I could see immediately that she was going to knock him to the ground and, once he was on his back, use her leverage to beat his body into the linoleum floor. Before she could do it, I darted forward and clamped her arm in mine, pulling her away from the boy.

"Unhand me!" she said, lashing out at me—but as soon as she saw who I was, her eyes widened in distress and she dropped to one knee, ashamed that she had almost attacked the very person she'd recently pledged her sword arm to.

Fae protocols—sometimes they could be useful.

"I am sorry, milady," she muttered in a rushed whisper.

I rolled my eyes. "Get up, Deirdre." I tried to help her up, but she wouldn't budge.

"What's going on?" the boy said, nervously laughing at the plateau before him. "What are we—in an episode of *Game of Thrones?*" He looked around him as if expecting Jon Snow to saunter by, and laughed again, this time derisively.

Deirdre ignored him, simply offering me the stone that had apparently caused all this ruckus. Up close, I saw what she was defending. My face flushed with rage as I stared at the fine carvings of the slab, making out the details of a cat-like eye with several medieval runes surrounding it.

The gargoyle from earlier … and the one good deed I'd done today. Seeing it, I guessed that either Mousey Girl did this—something I highly doubted, given her demeanor—or she'd abandoned the poor guy and he was attacked by a misguided human who thought that he was doing the world a service by killing it.

And now some idiot student wants to have a piece of the gargoyle's body as … what? … a freaking paperweight?

"Where did you get this?" I asked the boy.

"What's the big deal? It's just a piece of sto—"

"Where did you get this?" Now it was my turn to get in the kid's face.

His laughter had all but dried up in his throat. "I found it. In the stadium's parking lot."

"Stadium?" I pushed into him, demanding more.

"Yeah, you know, the football stadium just down the hill. The parking lot is a shortcut up to the dorms."

I hadn't been here long, but I did know about the stadium shortcut. If you entered through the parking lot and up the stairs into the stadium itself, you cut out the steepest part of the hill. A popular route for the lazy, drunk or overweight—or all three. Still, it didn't make sense that he'd found the remains of the gargoyle there. In the Student Ghetto, maybe, but the football stadium's parking lot? What was the gargoyle doing there?

I pushed him hard against the back wall of the laundry room. "Liar," I growled.

"No, I swear!" he said, his lips quivering with fear. "I was walking home, up Pine Street and through the lot, and that's where I found it. There were a bunch of stones piled there, like someone had smashed a statue or something. I sifted through it and found that piece and … and I thought it would look cool in my room."

"This isn't a piece of stone."

"What—what is it?"

I could feel Deirdre standing behind me now.

"You really don't understand," I said, "do you? This is part of a *gargoyle*. You know—stone guardians? They tend to live on castle turrets. What you picked up and so carelessly carried around with you is the equivalent of a severed head. This is part of something that was living, breathing … *thinking*. A creature who came to this place to make a better life for itself." I gripped the stone tighter as I clenched my teeth. "You should be reporting this to the police. You should be helping them find his killer. What you absolutely *shouldn't* be doing is bragging to that blond ditz about bringing home a trophy that used to be part of a *person*."

"Hey," she started, but I shot her a look that said it was not beneath me to beat her perfect little nose into her skull. She shut up.

I turned back to the guy. "This is a tragedy—not memorabilia. Do you understand that? Do you?"

He looked at me for a long, hard moment, his face so drained of expression that I couldn't tell if he was going to fly into a rage, cry or run away. The part of me that still yearned for the unbridled violence of my past wanted him to get angry. I wanted him to attack me so I could smash his smug face into the wall and then beat him senseless. But I was calm enough to know that wouldn't help. If anything, it would get me expelled, possibly arrested (again). Sure, that would solve my dropping-out-of-college conundrum, but it would also sow more discontent between humans and Others. So I just stared him down, not saying anything more, waiting for him to make his decision.

What he finally settled on was a macho "Screw you," followed by him grabbing the blonde's hand as he pulled her out of the room. She dropped her basket as they left, and I watched it teeter for a long moment, then finally settle on its base.

I looked down at my hand, at the face of a creature who only a couple of hours ago was sitting in Student Admin seeking to quit this place. *"GoneGodDamn it ... I got involved and convinced him to go with Mousy Girl because I thought they could get along. Idiot!"*

"No, milady," said my roommate, whom I'd forgotten was standing right behind me. "It is I who is the fool. I should have never engaged the ill-informed human. I should have—"

"Deirdre," I interrupted. The last thing I needed was a rehash of what had just happened. "Do you know how to give this gargoyle a proper burial?"

Deirdre hesitated, then nodded. "If I can learn his name, then yes."

His name—I had no idea what his name was. Trying to help, and I hadn't even bothered to ask his name. I didn't bother to ask any of their names. Yet another piece of proof that I wasn't here to connect ... I was just *here*.

Rubbing my fingers along the curves of this once-living statue, I thought about how I could find his name. Maybe when he went into Student Admin ... he must have signed in, right? That was a possibility. I sighed and handed Deirdre his cracked face. "I'll try to find that out for you. In the meantime ... take care of him?"

"As you command," she said.

I started out of the laundry room and toward my dorm. "One more thing," I said as I walked away. "Stop with all this 'as you command,' 'milady' and 'my sword arm is yours' stuff. People don't talk like that. Not on Earth, at least, and considering you're an Earthly being now, you've got to get with the program."

" 'Program'? " She tilted her head in confusion.

"Just act like everyone else. It's better that way."

I stepped into the hall and Deirdre followed me.

Walking into our room, I saw that much of the soil and grass still littered the floor, but at least it was *mostly* clean. Grumbling to myself,

I took off my shoes and jacket, put down my purse and, without getting into my pajamas, crawled into bed.

I closed my eyes, but could feel something—or, rather, some*one*—staring at me. Without opening my eyes, I said, "What is it, Deirdre?"

"You saw his body?"

"Whose?"

"The librarian's?"

I groaned. "How do you know about that?"

"It is now common knowledge."

"Which part?"

"That an Other killed the librarian—and that you bore witness to his death."

"Not exactly. The only thing I *bore* witness to was his dead body. I showed up after he had been killed. And there's no evidence it was an Other who killed him. That's just an assumption based on fear-driven stereotypes—bigotry."

"I see, mila— ... my friend."

I thought that was it, but when I didn't hear her move, I opened my eyes to see Deirdre slightly bent over, staring down at me.

"Is there something else, Deirdre?"

"Yes. There will be a candlelight vigil held in his honor. I wish to attend."

"So attend," I said.

"Will you attend with me?"

I thought about it. The Old Librarian was my friend—I think. I had only met him once, but I did like him. Attending would be appropriate. But after all that had happened, I figured it was best to never leave my dorm room again. I seemed to get in trouble when I did. Shaking my head, I said, "I don't think so. I'm tired and—"

"In the UnSeelie Court, vigils lasted forty days and forty nights, with the warrior class standing guard over the body, our swords always at the ready."

"What's your point?"

"Here on Earth, I do not believe that they observe the same customs."

"What gave you that clue?"

"This." She pulled out a flyer from her pocket. The same one that Justin had handed me earlier. "The invitation."

"It's not an in—" I started, then thought better of it. "Sorry, you were saying?"

"The invitation speaks of candles and invites people to speak. It also has several religious symbols decorating its borders. The rituals of this vigil will be different than the ones I know."

"Again, so …?"

"I require a human escort."

"I'm hardly human," I said.

"Then a being that understands human rituals," she said, evidently not getting that I was joking. "I fear that if I go alone, I will only make a fool of myself."

"So don't go."

She looked at me, as if hurt. "Vigils are a requirement for one such as I. It was our duty to attend all for whom an invitation had been issued."

She thought she was specially invited. And because of that, she was obligated to attend. Oh, brother … she'd have been a Latter-day Saint's dream come true before the GrandExodus.

I thought about explaining that flyers were just a thing humans did to disseminate information, but seeing the steel in her eyes, I knew she not only saw it as her duty to go—it was something she *wanted* to do.

"Attend," I said. "But don't take your sword."

She gave me a longing look.

"No swords, Deirdre. And you don't need an escort. Just do what everyone else does."

She began to blink rapidly, and if I hadn't seen this behavior before, I would have thought she was having a seizure. But rapid blinking was the fae's equivalent of pleading. She was—in her way—on her knees, begging me to come.

"No," I said.

More rapid blinks.

"I'm not going."

Now the blinks were not only faster but out of sync, too. How the hell was she doing that?

"You're not going to stop unless I agree, are you?"

She shook her head, maintaining her manic blinks.

"Fine, fine," I said. "We'll go. Satisfied?"

Deirdre stopped blinking and smiled.

"Good. Now if you don't mind …" I said, and pulled my duvet over my head.

"If I do not mind what?"

"Please be quiet and let me nap, Deirdre!"

The room went silent. Thank the GoneGods.

16

STICKS AND STONES HURT
WAAAAY LESS THAN WORDS

I woke up to Deirdre wearing my grass-green blouse, her hair tied back in a ponytail, with tiny lilacs in her hair and a laurel wreath on her head. She was watching the news on my iPad. I guess among her fae ethics, using my stuff without permission was nowhere in sight. I thought about reprimanding her, taking it away, but then I heard the Global News Montreal news anchor start his report with, "More mythical creatures being targeted in hate crimes."

I got out of bed and asked Deirdre to turn it up. Together, we watched in horror as two satyrs being carted away on a stretcher, a flash of an angel bleeding light on the sidewalk as police interviewed her, and three pixies crying as they were taken away in the back of a police car. What wasn't shown was the dead gargoyle—which kind of made sense. The police, like the kid in the Iron Man hoodie, would have mistaken him for a pile of rubble and not a body at a crime scene.

The anchor ended his report with, "Police theorize that these attacks are in response to the death of Dr. Dewey, who was brutally murdered by an unknown Other late last night," signing off after that.

"Dr. Dewey?"

"The librarian," Deirdre said. "Dewey was his surname."

Hearing his name felt like a slap in the face. All this time, I knew him as the "Old Librarian," and that put some distance between us. Now that I knew his name, much of that distance was lost.

I lifted my face to the ceiling, desperately trying to stop a tear from escaping. "What else is the news saying?"

Deirdre told me. It seemed that in the six hours or so that I had slept, there had been a half-dozen attacks on campus. All against Others. I guess the murder of the Old Librarian—uhh, Dr. Dewey—opened the floodgates of tension. Given how dangerous Others were supposed to be, there were a hell of a lot more Others being hurt at the hands of humans than humans being hurt by Others.

But isn't that how fear works? It turns aggressors into the righteous and victims into demons.

"This is just one report," Deirdre said. "There are other stories on other channels." A tiny tear ran down her cheek and fell on the iPad's screen.

"I know," I said, my own tear escaping.

"What can we do about it?"

"Nothing."

Deirdre sighed heavily.

"I'm sorry, Deirdre, but there's nothing to do. We just have to wait until the anger subsides and pray that the world comes to its senses."

"Pray? To whom?"

I didn't answer. There was no one to pray to. Everyone knew that.

Deirdre handed me the iPad and stood up. "Perhaps tonight's vigil will help heal some wounds. Perhaps—"

"You can't go to the vigil, Deirdre! You'll be in real danger there."

She gave me a look like I was the crazy one to consider *not* going.

"Look," I explained, "there will be a lot of angry people there. Angry humans. Humans who will want to take out their frustration on an Other just like you. There's no way. I'm not going and neither are you."

"But I was invited. As a fae warrior, I cannot—"

"You're no longer a fae warrior. You are a mortal creature living in a world without gods."

"But … but …" She bunched her hands together, holding them so tight that her fingers turned white with the effort. "I am *fae*." Two more tears escaped and rolled down her cheeks. "Oberon and Titania may have abandoned us … the UnSeelie Court and Planes of Forever Green may no longer be … but that does not make me any less fae than I was. I am fae. I will always be fae."

With those words, she dried her eyes and looked at the clock. "The hour is near," she said. "I will attend the vigil—with or without my human guide."

I'd been around the fae enough to know that once they made up their minds, nothing short of divine intervention could discourage them. And since we were all out of that, I sighed and pulled an old poncho out of my drawer. "OK—we'll go. But you can't dress like that."

* * *

As we made our way down the hill to campus, I expected to see the streets filled with people shouting anti-Other chants, some fights, the air thick with tension. Anger.

Hate.

But that wasn't the case at all. Instead, Deirdre and I found dozens of students carrying cardboard signs that read various flowery stuff like:

OTHERS DESERVE THEIR PLACE.
LOVE STILL MATTERS.
WE MUST WELCOME THE MYTHICAL REFUGEES INTO OUR HOMES.

And once we got into the vigil itself, I saw students crying, more signs, a picture of the Old Librarian surrounded by flowers and candles. The hate simply wasn't here. Well, at least it felt like that …

But I couldn't shake the feeling that this was just the calm before the storm.

* * *

We started to make our way through the crowds because, as Deirdre put it, it was our duty to light a candle in his honor. I thought it was enough we showed up, but who was I to argue with fae logic?

Whatever, I thought as we wove through the sea of bodies. *As long as we make it there and back without drawing too much attention to our—*

"Ms. Darling," I heard a voice say. "It's good to see you here."

I turned to see Detective Sarah Wilcox standing behind me. And right next to her was a boy in a hoodie who looked like he'd much rather be in a million other places than on this field at this time.

"Detective Wilcox. Good to see you here, too," I said. "And hi, Nate. How's it going?"

Nate shrugged.

"OK," I said, wondering what his problem was. "Is Justin here, too?"

Nate didn't look up, simply pointing at the founder statue. "He's setting up for his big speech."

"I see that you're already acquainted with my cousin," Wilcox said.

"I am. Sort of. He mostly made fun of me. Something about *Weird Girl* and his friend Justin."

"Is that true, dear cousin?" Wilcox said, pinching his cheeks in that exaggerated way you did to kids.

Nate withdrew in anger, slapping her hand away. "Bitch," he said.

"Excuse me?" Detective Wilcox said, seriousness flooding her face.

"Not you—*her,*" Nate said.

Now it was my turn. "Excuse me?" Deirdre took a step forward, but I held out a hand. "I can handle this. Now, again, excuse me?"

Nate looked up, finally pulling his hoodie off his head. "You heard me. *Bitch.*" He took a step forward.

"What is your problem?"

He pointed at the Other Studies Library and whispered, "My

cousin here says you're not the killer, but I saw you with those hockey players."

"I was defending that poor Other beggar. And besides, all I did was give them a bloody nose. I didn't string them up or—"

That's when Nate pushed me. And I don't mean a gentle, get-out-of-my-way nudge. It was a full-on shove, and since I wasn't expecting it, I landed hard on my ass.

Deirdre immediately got between us, and if I had waited a second longer, she might have shoved him back. Being shoved by a human might get you on the floor, but being shoved by a pissed-off changeling—that was likely to send you to the next block.

"Don't, Deirdre. It's not worth it." Deirdre gave me a confused look as I clambered back to my feet, so I added—just for good measure, "Against human protocol to fight at a vigil. Nate here dishonors the Old Librarian—"

"Dr. Dewey," Deirdre said.

"Yes, Dr. Dewey." I gave Nate a cold, hard stare, then flashed the fakest smile I could muster. Turning to Detective Wilcox, I noticed she hadn't moved. She must have been just as shocked as I was. "I don't know what your problem is, Nate," I said, "but I *liked* Dr. Dewey. And even if I didn't, I would have never—"

That's when Nate spit in my face.

I lunged at him, and if it hadn't been for Deirdre taking my *No fighting at vigils* comment seriously, it would have been Nate knocked on his ass. That, and Wilcox stepping between us. From her expression, I could tell she didn't know if she should hit me or reprimand Nate.

Pointing a threatening finger in Nate's face, I said, "This isn't over."

I pulled Deirdre close and we made our way to the memorial. I glanced over my shoulder to see Nate and Wilcox watching me walk away. Wilcox still had a puzzled look on her face, but Nate …

Nate was smiling.

* * *

We passed by students strumming guitars, singing hymns, reciting poetry, lighting candles—all paying homage to a man who virtually none of them knew. And yet I could sense that their misery was genuine. They truly felt the loss. Why? How could they lament the loss of someone they never knew? Was it fear that something happened so close to them? Fear that if it happened to him, it could happen to them?

Or maybe it was something else ... a human thing. Humans crying for humans? I doubted that, too. I'd seen so many wars and random killing—hell, I'd committed many of those—and I'd never seen this kind of reaction.

No, there was something else going on. But what it was, I could not tell.

And then I saw Deirdre crying and knew that it wasn't just humans who were being affected. Whatever they felt, Deirdre felt it, too.

"Wrongful, violent death shakes us all," I thought.

Deirdre nodded in agreement.

OK—so we all felt his death. Very well, then ... let me pay my respects. We got near the frozen image of him; looking into his kind blue eyes, I knelt down and picked up a candle that had gone out and lit it from the flame of another.

I stared at his image for a long moment, wondering how my life would be different here if he were alive and well—and my boss. I wondered if our friendship would have grown. I suspected it would. After all, we'd be spending a lot of time together, shelving books, categorizing the museum collection, taking care of the old building's needs. That would have been a good thing—but now it was gone.

And soon, I'll be gone, too, I thought, shaking my head and crying.

* * *

A hand touched my shoulder. I whirled to see Egya standing behind me.

"Why," I said, "do you always show up when I least want you to? Which is to say, why do you show up at all?"

But Egya wasn't paying attention to me. He was pointedly looking everywhere else but at me, his eyes shifting back and forth.

"What is it?" I said, whispering now and drawing closer.

"Look," he said.

I turned to see that most of the people standing immediately around the memorial were looking at us, no longer speaking, just staring in silence. Their tears were turning into curled lips and clenched fists. But why would they direct their anger at me? Was it because I had been there at his death? How could they know who I was? As far as any of them knew, I was just another student paying her respects. I scanned the area around me for Deirdre. She was standing about ten feet away, under the canopy of the old oak tree. Her hood was still over her head and she was looking down, mournful and lost in her own grief.

"Sheesh," I said. "What's everyone's problem?"

"Come," Egya said softly. "Walk with me and watch their eyes."

We walked over to Deirdre. As we did, everyone who was within ten yards of us looked up at our passing and stared, hate painting their faces. But that wasn't the strangest thing about this. As people fell outside of the ten yards, they'd stop staring at us and continue their conversations as if they hadn't been trying to bore holes in us with their eyes.

"A curse," I whispered.

"Strange guess for someone who is just a human girl," Egya said. Then he shook his head. "This is not a curse—there is too much emotion. *This* … is a hex."

I swallowed, digesting what he'd just said.

A hex was serious business. Think of them as souped-up versions of curses, the difference being a curse was a general suggestion that things "go wrong" for its intended victim—bad luck, disease, poverty, lost love, even death—but because it was just a suggestion, a gentle nudge that things fall apart, it can take forever to happen, if it happens at all. It is entirely possible the intended victim's immunity (as in the case of disease) is strong enough to ward off the curse. Or perhaps the target is incredibly lucky or rich or in love, and thus the curse falls flat.

A *hex* was something else entirely. The right hex, with the right amount of time burnt for the proper amount of magic, not only causes bad luck, disease, poverty, lost love or even death—you can get really specific with its terms and conditions. Say you wanted the victim to die in a spectacular fashion, maybe get hit by a bus. No problem. The victim will find themselves wandering into a highway for no reason at all. Lost love? The intended victim will happily take photos of themselves with a sheep (in the, erm, biblical sense) and send it to their lover with the subject line *I've found someone who fulfills me in ways you never could.*

Hexes were the Terminators of curses.

I closed my eyes. Even when I couldn't see the people glaring at us, I could still feel their rage. But to say they were merely angry at us would be wrong. The hatred they focused on us was palpable. You could literally feel it. And I don't mean that as a euphemism or an exaggeration. I mean that making eye contact with them created a sense of tension that felt as if someone had wrapped a garroting thread around us and was pulling. Hard.

But I couldn't let Egya know that I—someone who was just a girl— knew the difference between hexes and curses, so mustering all the acting skills I'd learned from daytime soaps, I widened my eyes. In a worried, trembling voice, I asked, "What's the difference?"

He smirked at this question—evidently not believing my *Days of Our Lives* shock. "One is bad. One is terrible. But at least hexes have one thing to our advantage. They don't last long. Too much burnt time is needed to keep them up."

"Why us?" I whispered.

He cocked a thumb toward the library. "Not us ... *you.*"

"Me? How do you know?"

"I've been following their eyes. Always trained on you. Not your changeling friend. Not me. You."

I scanned the crowd as we reached Deirdre. Egya was right—all eyes were on me. I nodded. "OK, it's me. But why?"

Egya shrugged. "Isn't it obvious? You disrupted the killer's ritual and he wants you to suffer for it. This killer of yours is a vengeful spirit."

"But if I am the focal point, then why aren't you affected? Or Deirdre? Why aren't you two staring at me like you wanna spill my guts?"

He shrugged again. "Because we know you."

I gave him a look. "Hardly."

"We know you enough to know you aren't our enemy. But they—" he pointed to the crowd "—*they* don't know you from Eve … and that is all that is needed to turn a stranger into an enemy."

"Fine. Let's say I believe you. What kind of 'fun' exactly did I interrupt?"

"Not fun. *Ritual*. Do you really think Dr. Dewey was strung up for fun, just-a-girl?"

"Don't call me that—and yes, why not?"

Egya narrowed his eyes like he was trying to figure me out. "What kind of killers would go to such lengths 'just for fun'? No—the killer was performing a ritual, preparing the body for something … bigger."

The thought that the killer wasn't just maiming the librarian for his or her twisted amusement hadn't really crossed my mind. To be honest, I used to kill for fun … I guess I assumed that if I did so, then most killers would be like me.

"What ritual?" I asked.

"I have no idea. And we don't have time to consider this now." Egya pointed at two boys who were starting to walk toward us. They were two of the three hockey players from yesterday—the ones who had been picking on Mergen—the big one with the now thrice-broken nose and the short one with the unfortunate ponytail. "Their hate will turn to rage. The rage that will be directed at you—and anyone they consider to be your friend." He gestured at Deirdre, and I could see the third hockey player now heading toward her.

I walked over to Deirdre and whispered, "Pull your hood on tight and get rid of those leaves. We're leaving."

"Why?" she gurgled between her own tears. "We just got here and I have yet to sing 'The Solemn Ode to the Dead.'"

"We've got to go. Now. Move it."

Deirdre might have been a bubbling mess of emotions, but she was, first and foremost, a trained warrior. And as a trained warrior, you learn to trust the instincts of those around you—especially those you have pledged your sword arm.

Without bothering to wipe away her tears, she plucked the leaves from her head, dropping them to the grass at her feet, and swept her hood over her head.

"Good," I muttered. "Let's go." Grabbing her by the arm, I guided her toward the main gate. It was only a few feet in front of us when the two hockey players from earlier blocked our way.

"The Other lover," Broken Nose said. His voice was comically nasal with that plaster cast covering his schnoz. "What are you doing here?"

"Same as everyone else," I growled. "Paying my respects." I tried to push past them.

Without warning, Ponytail pulled at my ponytail—ironic, really—at which point Deirdre grabbed his wrist and squeezed.

"Ahh—"

But before he could let out a full scream, I covered his mouth. "Deirdre, let him go," I said.

She did as I asked.

Broken Nose tried to intervene, but I put a finger up to his lips, just touching the bottom of his casted nose so that his eyes watered with pain. I said, "Not here and not now. I will not let Dr. Dewey be disrespected by the lot of you. So if you want me, come get me. Bring your brood—" I gestured around us with my chin and suddenly saw that it wasn't just the three boys I'd seen walking toward us. Three more of their hockey friends had joined them ... plus, there were a lot more students ready to join the fight all around us. I gulped and repeated, "Bring your brood. We'll be waiting in the alleyway behind the bookstore."

I held on to Ponytail's mouth while Broken Nose considered this. Before he could object, I added, "Besides—look around you. See all the campus security? We don't want them interrupting a good fight, do we?"

I pointed to several security guards mulling about.

Broken Nose looked around and nodded. "Behind the campus bookstore," he agreed, a cocky smile creeping in the corners of his lips. "How do I know you'll be there?"

"Because," I said, finally pushing Ponytail away and brushing past them. "You can follow me there right now."

"Brave girl," Egya said, pulling in close to me.

"Not brave," I muttered to him as we walked through the crowd. "If hexes work the way I think they do, a fight in this place will only mean we have to face off against more and more people as it grows in strength. We can take care of a half-dozen testosterone-fueled idiots, can't we?"

Egya snorted in answer.

"But," I continued, "I have another reason why I want an alleyway showdown. If this is a hex, then the killer must be somewhere nearby, right? He—"

"Or she."

"—or *she* may even join the fight. It will be easier to pick him or her out behind the bookstore."

"Pick him or her out as we're being stomped to a pulp," Egya said. "Excellent plan."

"Oh, don't be so dramatic. We have a changeling warrior with us."

Egya looked over at Deirdre, who was cracking her fingers, Bruce Lee–style, as she walked just behind us. "Indeed," he said, grinning. "Indeed, we do."

"Besides," I said as we made our way to the main gate, "I meant what I said. Dr. Dewey deserves more than having a fight break out at his memorial."

Just as we made our way off campus, a speaker scratched, cutting through the general noise of the crowd. Looking back, I saw Justin holding a mic attached to a portable amp. He was standing on the rim of the water-fountain base, the founder's statue beside him. He suddenly looked like some ancient Roman god giving the opening commencement for a spring festival.

And somehow, as if the fates were conspiring against me, our eyes met as Egya continued to pull me away. I was walking out on his speech … and he saw me doing it.

Maybe I was *also* cursed?

17

UP, UP AND AWAY!

The main campus was a roughly square gated area that covered a dozen or so acres in the middle of the city. Immediately surrounding campus were several buildings that played supportive roles to the education of a future generation. School-supply shops, buildings that housed more classrooms, the smaller libraries or study rooms, and student cafés, restaurants and bars.

The bookstore was the largest building adjacent to campus; an alleyway cut between it and the Faculty of Management building. Since the alleyway was between the bookstore and the lamest faculty building, I figured it would be empty.

I figured wrong.

Mergen was sitting there leafing through a basket of old books he probably got for pennies at some charity shop. From the way he scanned the pages, I figured he wasn't finding much to eat in Harlequin romances, old Westerns and hard-boiled detective novels. Still, he wasn't looking as emaciated as he'd been just earlier today, so I guess those old trash novels weren't *completely* devoid of Truth.

That, or he was still getting nourishment from my little outburst earlier.

Mergen looked up as we walked by, and I considered ignoring

him, but quickly realized that wouldn't work. The hex was on me—me ... and anyone considered my ally. Three of the mob following us had been on the receiving end when I defended the pale white rider, and one of them was sporting a broken nose from it. They'd see him as a bonus.

"Follow me," I said. "Your life might just depend on it."

"Mmm," Mergen said, licking his lips. "Yes, it just might."

* * *

I drew the crowd into the alleyway, careful to pull them into the far end so that we—as in, my "gang"—were actually spilling out into the other exit. That way, I figured, they couldn't sneak up on us and block off our escape route. I was hoping that this way we would get there and, seeing who showed up, I'd have a fairly good sense of who the killer was. We'd fight—maybe. Normally I'd think this would digress into some posturing, a bit of blustering bravado, insults and maybe a few shoves, before fizzling out into nothing. After all, these kids didn't want to get into a fight any more than we wanted to have one. Unless maybe their leader was going for a record and wanted his nose broken again.

But we were hexed—which means they were compelled to attack.

No worries, I thought—I'd already seen how Egya could handle himself, and Deirdre was a born warrior. Mergen was my only concern, and he was the freaking avatar of the Turkish god of war and wisdom.

"I think this is far enough," said Broken Nose, and in this dark alley, that ridiculous nasal voice was even more comical. "We don't want to be on the main road and attract the wrong kind of attention, right?"

So let's let the blustering bravado begin, I thought.

Egya and a couple of the hockey minions chuckled at this. So they weren't so far under the spell that they didn't see the absurdity of the situation. *Good,* I thought, silently this time, *I can work with that.*

I stared at an asshole who, when unhexed, had wanted to pummel a poor defenseless Other for the crime of being different. Hexed asshole and unhexed asshole were pretty much the same guy—just minus any inhibition, common sense or fear. A fight was coming. I knew it. He knew it. Everyone here knew it. Which meant there were really only two questions left to be answered.

Was the guy (or gal) responsible for the hex in the crowd?

And how long until my side ran?

I scanned the crowd. As far as I could tell, everyone was human. A hex—as powerful as it was—needed magic. And since magic had left with the gods, a human conjuror was out. Sure, in the old days, a human witch, shaman, warlock or mage could have cast a spell like this, but he (or she) would have sold their soul to a demon, fae or whatever malevolent spirit said spellcaster ascribed to. But those days were gone (as was evident by my lost appetite for blood), so that meant the caster would have to be an Other.

And there were no Others in the crowd.

The only Others here were on my side, and despite desperately wanting to be human—with all their idiosyncrasies and pettiness—I was on theirs.

All I saw were the three assholes from yesterday and three more of their hockey friends, a group of cheerleaders, four goth kids (of everyone I saw, you'd think they'd be on our side at least) and—crap—one of Justin's frat brothers. I didn't know his name, but he had been there when Nate teased us.

Of everyone here, he was the only one who knew me—well, knew *of* me. He knew his O^3 Bro and I were flirting and that he'd have a lot of explaining to do if he went back to the dorm with my blood on his hands. Maybe I could use that.

"So," I said, "how does this start?"

"That's a great question," Broken Nose answered. "Since it's going to end with your funeral, and since civility didn't leave with the gods, I'll let *you* tell me how this all starts."

"We could *not* do this," I offered.

"Oh, no," he said, sneering. "This is happening."

Mergen affirmed this by smacking his lips in agreement. Guess this guy ate Truth even when it was being served up with a beating.

"Why?" I said, ignoring the Truth of the situation. "Come on—you have to feel that this is wrong, don't you?" I gestured at the crowd. "Why do you all hate me so much? Most of you don't even know me. And as for you—the only person who kind of knows me—" I pointed at Justin's friend "—am I really that bad of a person that I deserve what's about to happen?"

Reasoning with the angry mob—if only Frankenstein, Dracula, Quasimodo or the Beast had thought of trying. They probably had ... and then took one look into the mob's rage-filled eyes and opted for the fight-or-flight options.

Justin's friend gave me a regretful look before lowering his head. "Ah, Justin ... Justin really likes you."

I looked at Mergen for confirmation, but he just shrugged. I guess when it comes to matters of the heart, Truth is murky. *"Still,"* I thought, *"given that this guy is being compelled to hurt me, I'm going to give his revelation the benefit of the doubt—Justin likes me. Yay!"*

"Ahh, Kat—this is not the time," Egya whispered in my ear.

"I said that out loud, didn't I?"

"Indeed."

"Sorry," I muttered. I pointed at the O^3 Bro. "So if Justin, your *friend*, likes me, can I be as bad as you evidently feel about me? Or maybe, just maybe, there's something wrong going on here."

He shook his head, then nodded. "Maybe ... It's all so confusing." He hit his forehead with the palm of his hand. "So muddled."

"Friends—lend me your ears."

"Kat ..." Egya whispered. "What are you doing?"

"Quoting Shakespeare."

"You're quoting a guy who got stabbed multiple times by his friends."

"Whatever—just shush and let me work my charm." I turned back to the crowd, lifted my left hand and placed my right hand over my heart. I called out, "You do not wish to hurt me—us. Don't you see? Dr. Dewey's killer wants to distract us by causing distrust and anger. There is an evil spell afoot, cast to sow the seeds of distrust and anger. Let us not give him—or her—the satisfaction. Let us walk away and foil this evil plan."

I turned to my friends. Mergen groaned, but Deirdre was nodding in approval.

Egya, on the other hand, eyed me with confusion. "Why are you speaking like that?"

"Gravitas—more likely to break the spell with it than without."

"Is it?" he asked. Then, grabbing me with lightning-fast reflexes, he pulled me several inches to the right just as a beer bottle flew by. "Perhaps not as effective as you think."

I turned to see the crowd shifting their weight from foot to foot as they prepared to advance. Looking over at Justin's Bro, the only one who expressed doubt, I saw that he had traded his confused eyes for clenched fists. He cracked his knuckles in that *I got a tough job ahead of me* sort of way and took a step forward.

So much for talking them out of this.

"OK," I said. "Time for Plan B."

"Plan B?" Deirdre asked, stepping forward so that she stood shoulder to shoulder with me.

"Yep, Plan B." I kicked Broken Nose in the shin and, as he went down, I punched him in the broken nose, breaking the plaster cast. The pain knocked him out cold. I looked at the remaining seventeen people and assessed my options.

Then I turned around and ran.

* * *

Have you ever been chased by an angry mob through a modern city that prides itself on being tolerant? If not, you're missing out.

There's a certain brand of ire that rolls off all the citizens like waves of heat as you run past them. First, they watch you, confusion painting their faces, perhaps saying to one another:

"Why are two humans and two Others being chased?"

"Is this right?"

"Aren't we welcoming to Others?"

"Should we call someone?"

But then, as you pass by them and the hex takes hold, that confusion becomes certainty:

These four are guilty of something—not sure what, but that doesn't matter.

What matters is they are captured—brought to justice.

Better yet—dealt with.

These four are clearly evil!

And finally: *The mob chasing them will need help. Our help.*

Which effectively meant the angry mob grew every time we passed a pedestrian, someone sitting outside or a dog walker. I even saw two drivers abandon their cars just so they could chase us on foot.

We ran out of the alley and up toward the mountain. It was night, and I figured that the best place to lose them was up where there were no streetlamps, limited population to fall under the hex and lots of trees casting moon shadows to hide under. Still, that meant running uphill and past Gerts, the campus bar, where a bunch of students who had opted to skip the vigil were standing outside smoking. Before we even passed them, they were flicking away their cigarettes or pocketing their vaping devices and moving to block our way. I had to knee one of them in the—*ahem*—family jewels, and elbow another's nose to get past.

How many noses does a girl have to break to get left the hell alone?

Egya chose a more elegant solution—he jumped on a parked car and used the height advantage to jump clear over them. Elegant, indeed, especially when compared to Deirdre, who opted to clothesline several guys before they even had a chance to pocket their lighters. Mergen, however, was less suited to get past them. Deirdre and I had to double back, flattening two girls who were literally trying to tie him up with their cardigans.

We got past them just as the main mob caught up.

"We need to get out of the city!" Egya yelled. "Up there." He pointed at the beginning of the mountain's treeline. "If we could just get in there before they tear us apart, we might be able to lose them."

We ran and ran some more, until finally we arrived. There was our potential salvation, a neat line of trees heralding the entrance to a vast forest—and all we had to do was cross a four-lane road … that was currently bumper-to-bumper traffic.

Perfect!

"Jump over the hoods!" I yelled, taking a leaf from Egya's book.

Egya nodded appreciatively, but Deirdre didn't immediately understand my reasoning and opted to run between two cars. Before she even got through, the white reverse lights of the lead car lit up and the back car's engine revved. The two cars collided into each other as they tried to pinch her between back and front bumpers.

"Deirdre!" I screamed.

Fortunately, changelings have lightning-fast reflexes. She managed to jump straight up and onto the back car's hood before she was caught. The driver, who, under the powers of the hex, also had fast reflexes, threw his car into reverse. Deirdre fell. Then he floored the car again, trying to throw her into the car in front of his.

Deirdre managed to get to her feet just as I jumped onto my first hood, where that driver did the same thing, trying to knock me off my feet.

This was the worst game of Frogger I'd ever played—and given that I was helping Mergen cross, it wasn't loading well for me … at this pace, the crowd would catch up and tear us to shreds.

So I did the only thing I could think of—I jumped back off the car and opened the driver's door. I yanked the driver out and, pushing Mergen through to the passenger's side, made an impromptu tunnel for us.

Then I grabbed the next driver and, using a kickboxing move I learned in Bangkok, swiped her feet and knocked her to the floor of the car. I gestured to Mergen to move his ass and we burrowed through the second car.

Two lanes crossed. *Frogger Level 50% Complete.* Only two more cars and we'd be at the treeline.

Except, by now, the two other cars were savvy to my strategy and had simply locked their doors to foil me.

Mergen and I were trapped, with the angry mob only yards behind us. I was looking for an escape when I heard a deep honk and saw that, several cars back, Egya had hijacked a city bus.

He slammed on the accelerator and the two cars in front of us smashed into each other, which stopped the cars from doing their back-and-forth trick. He'd also managed to use the sheer size of the bus to do the same thing to the cars in the fourth and final lane. This made jumping over their hoods relatively safe. Mergen and I, thankful for the assist, wasted no time getting across the other two lanes over the tops of the cars.

"Thanks!" I yelled as we made it to the treeline. Egya honked his reply.

Once inside, we ran up the middle of the woods. My plan was to get to Beaver Lake, where there were a few buildings for us to break into and hide. I turned to see the angry mob bursting through the treeline. We were only about forty feet ahead of them, but at least, being in this brush, we were out of their line of sight.

"Come on—let's move," I whispered.

Deirdre grabbed my arm and stopped me. "No," she said. "I have a better idea."

"What are you doing? We've got to keep moving," I said.

But Deirdre didn't budge. She just placed a calm finger over her lips, shushing me. She faced the road. I could hear the angry mob only yards away. A few more seconds and they'd be parallel with us. All it would take was one of them to look to their right and we'd be sunk.

But Deirdre just stood stock-still, almost defiantly so. I suddenly worried that she was planning to do something stupid and attack the human mob. But Deirdre didn't attack. She ... swooned—as in lightly swayed back and forth, her feet planted firmly in place. Then, fanning out her fingers and twirling them so it looked like she was playing some invisible piano, she began to hum.

"Deirdre! Be quiet," I whispered harshly, taking a step forward. If she wasn't going to shut up, I'd have to shut her up.

Egya stopped me. "Kat ... look." He pointed at the ground.

What I saw was nothing short of a miracle.

The earth around us began to move. No, *move* was the wrong word … moving implies that something shifts from one place to another. The brush didn't just *shift*. It grew and expanded and intertwined itself until it formed a canopy in front of us that blocked the view from the road—but what was even more odd was that we could still *see* the road. Like window blinds, the leaves had angled themselves so we had a one-way view out while blocking the view in. And what was most spectacular about what was happening was the brush didn't make any noise as it twisted and angled, grew and intertwined.

It was utterly silent.

The angry mob ran past us, completely unaware. I could hear Ponytail call out, "They must be at the lake." The rallying cry of determined and violent humans followed, and we heard the scamper of feet continue along the path.

After a long minute, the footsteps faded into the darkness, and we were alone.

Deirdre turned to me, smiling, proud of what she'd just done. "Camouflage—fae-style," she said simply.

I nodded curtly. "How long?"

Deirdre tilted her head to one side in confusion.

"You burnt time, right? To create the magic that did this?"

She nodded.

"How long?"

She didn't answer.

"How long?" I growled.

"Twelve hours."

I stared at her. "Twelve *hours*? Do you know what you can do with twelve hours? And you wasted them—threw that precious time away —and for what? We could have outrun them."

"Kat," Egya interjected, "I disagree. We were pretty far away from them for a while, and we're even farther away now, but they're still an angry mob. Even outside of the hex. They wouldn't have let us just run away."

I looked around at my hapless crew. "That doesn't justify what Deirdre did, Egya. She wasted twelve hours of her life. For nothing."

Mergen groaned.

"Shut up—just because you don't like the taste of something, doesn't make it a lie."

Mergen smacked his lips.

"We could have outrun them," I repeated, my rage bubbling.

Deirdre stared down at the ground.

"Kat," Egya said. "The girl did what she thought was best. She sacrificed her time to save us. You should be more—"

"What? Grateful? Grateful that I'm on top of a volcano with you? Grateful that someone is trying to kill me? Grateful that my fellow students want to string me up?"

"The hex will wear off by morning."

"But how do you know? You just said they're outside the range of the hex. So how do you know?"

Egya's cold glare was all I got as an answer.

"Fine—it will wear off by morning. What do we do until then?"

Without turning around, Egya pointed up toward the huge neon cross at the top of the hill, to the right of where the mob had run. "We rest."

"Oh, great," I said, pushing past him. "We rest." I trekked up the hill toward the neon cross and my bed for the night.

Here I was—an ex-vampire—sitting under a Christian crucifix, the symbol that I had feared for three hundred years and now used as sanctuary, on top of a GoneGodsDamned volcano and waiting for dawn so that an angry mob hexed out of their minds wouldn't kill me.

Great advice to stay, Medusa, I thought, not caring if it was in my head or aloud.

As I reached the cross, I wondered if there was a worse place for me to be.

END OF PART 3

PART IV
INTERMISSION

"This may come off as arrogant ... but I know why the gods left."

Cue the dramatic pause, look around the audience, make eye contact. That's very important—eye contact. That's the one commonality between Others and humans—neither group can ignore eye contact. Then take a deep breath. Give them your best wicked smile. You know the one—the golden smile that has gotten you your way so many times before. The smile that says you are smart but down-to-earth. Beautiful, but somehow still approachable. Young, but wise.

"I know what many of you are thinking. How do I know something that so many scholars, philosophers, scientists, politicians and theologians don't know? The answer is simple—they know, too. They just don't have the balls to say it."

Cue the fencing—just so the audience knows there is no escape.

"The gods left because we disappointed them."

Begin the incantation. Evoke Huitzilopochtli. Evoke Shang Ti, Moloch, Kū, Re—even Yahweh. After all, the Old Testament was full of animal sacrifices. What is a human but an upgrade?

"They left because we forgot who they were."

Push the scared little students into the center of the field. Then randomly point at someone young and frail—but pick carefully. You need the first sacrifice to be a screamer. Wait silently as the first sacrifice is tied to the tabernacle—the stone lip of the dried-up fountain. Once the virgin is secure, resume your speech.

"They left because we forgot who we were."

Pull out the knife. The virgin will scream, so wait it out. If he or she doesn't stop after, say, ten seconds, gag them. Remember: at this point, the party will probably think this is all part of the show. It won't be until the blood starts flowing that they'll realize what's truly going on. Realize that they are all doomed to the same fate.

"Well, it's time to remind us all—god and mortal alike—just who and what we are."

Run the knife's tip along the virgin's body. Take it slow.

"Once that happens, they'll come back."

Stab, stab, stab.

"Did I mention my speech was going to kill?"

18

ON A HILL, BENEATH A NEON CROSS, WAITING FOR DAWN

*D*ay One of University: Witness a gruesome murder and defeat a giant bulldog.

Day Two of University: Spend the morning hours being interrogated by a detective and the nighttime hours being chased by an angry mob.

And before Day Three even begins, I'm hiding out beneath a giant neon cross crowning an inactive volcano. My companions include a changeling, the physical representation of Mergen the Turkish god of War and Wisdom—a creature who feeds on, might I add, the Truth—and some guy from Ghana who thinks he knows me.

"I do know you," Egya called out. "I know what you were and who you are."

GoneGodsDamn it—talking out loud again. "Private thought," I yelled back.

"I also know what you will become if you don't face your past."

"Oh, and what's that?" I hoisted myself off the mesh fence that surrounded the base of the cross and walked up to Egya. I might not have had my vampiric strength anymore, but I still knew karate, kung fu, Krav Maga, Brazilian jujitsu, as well as Scottish and aikido-based swordplay ... and I was looking for a fight.

Egya made a growling noise. Not like a dog. This sounded more like someone trying to suppress a laugh. A menacing, scary, soul-shaking laugh.

Deirdre stood behind me. "If you lay a hand on Lady Darling, I shall—"

"Yeah, yeah," Egya said, stepping back. "I won't touch her. I don't hit girls."

Mergen groaned at this, clutching his stomach in pain.

"Sentient lie detector," I said, pointing at the avatar.

"Fine," he said. "I don't hit girls … unless in the heat of battle, and said girl—" he pointed at me "—is an ex—"

"Don't you say it," I warned.

"—something-or-Other," Egya said, giving emphasis to that last word purposefully, "who is more than capable of defending herself. But I would never, ever hurt the defenseless or weak."

At this Mergen hummed and rubbed his belly in satisfaction.

I looked at Mergen, the sentient lie detector. How can that be the Truth? I thought.

"I'm not the hapless agent of chaos you think I am," Egya said. "Believe it or not, I want to help you."

Mergen licked his lips.

"See?" Egya said, pointing at Mergen.

"Help me? How? You mean like you did on campus?"

"I saved you."

"Again—how? Were you the one who had to re-break a nose that probably looks like a dumpster fire by now?"

"If it wasn't for me, you wouldn't have noticed the hex. And before you say anything—we all know you know exactly what a hex is … so don't play stupid with us."

Mergen sucked on his fingers one at a time, as if licking off barbecue sauce.

"You—" I pointed at the ghostly white avatar "—stop that. And you …" I looked back at Egya. "Why do you want to help me so badly?"

"Because," Egya said, "I know the cost of running from your past."

"I'm not running from anything."

"So that wasn't you going to Student Admin to drop out just two days into the semester?"

"I don't know what you're talking about!"

Mergen groaned and made a face like he had just accidentally drunk sour milk.

Deirdre looked at me, a look of hurt surprise on her face. "You are leaving?"

"No."

Mergen spat on the ground.

"I mean, yes."

I looked at Mergen, who continued to make a disapproving face.

"Maybe," I said.

At that, Mergen smiled.

"I haven't decided yet," I admitted. "But it's hard. I mean ..." I gestured around us. "This is only my third night here."

"It will get easier," Egya said. "You are only beginning your journey."

That really annoyed me. "Look here, Yoda," I said. "You can pretend to be the wise little sage that knows more about me than I know about myself, and you might have once upon a time been a were-dog—"

"Hyena."

"Were-pain-in-my-ass! Whatever you were, you're not that anymore. Now you're a human. A human like me. A stupid, worthless, broken human!" I cried out.

I don't know what happened exactly, but saying those words unleashed something in me. I started sobbing, still speaking between gasps. "It's just so hard. I mean—one minute you're—a supernatural predator that eats people—and the next—you're just—people."

I walked over to the mesh fence and looked up at the cross, basking in its neon halo. I calmed down, taking deep breaths and wiping the tears from my face. "Not too long ago, the sight of a cross would have sent me running. Its power protected those who believed in it from monsters like me."

Deirdre walked up behind me and put a hand on my shoulder. "A symbol that offers protection for those who wish it to."

I nodded. "But now, here, under this monstrous thing, I feel … nothing. Neither fear nor comfort. To me, this cross is just a piece of decoration on top of a hill."

"But, Lady Kat, is that not a good thing?" Deirdre drew in close. "This symbol can no longer cast its oppressive shadow over you. You are free."

"But that's just the thing. I don't feel happy, I don't feel free. I don't feel anything. About this cross, about being human again, about—" I stopped myself.

There was a long silence before Deirdre, the fae pain-in-my-ass, asked a question I did not have the courage to ask myself.

"Lady Kat, are you without … pain?"

I nodded.

Deirdre straightened her back and lowered her hands to her side so she resembled a tree trunk without branches—the fae's body language for concern or worry. "That is not good, Lady Kat. We fae believe that true life resides in the throes of emotion, be it comforting or adversarial."

Tears spilled down my face once more. "When we vampires became human, there was a lot of confusion. We lost our fangs, our powers and superhuman strength and senses. And we also lost our need to drink human blood. This caused us more confusion than you might think. For one thing, all the horrible things we did when we were demons came flooding back to us. Being human meant having a human conscience. And a conscience is a heavy burden.

"Most of us—at least among the ex-vampires I spoke to—decided on two things. One, we'd do our best to atone for what we had done. And two, we'd try to forgive ourselves. After all, it was the demon within us that killed all those people. And that demon's gone now. That has to count for something."

I had been staring up at the cross once more, but now I turned and looked back at everyone. "Well, it doesn't, and I will say one thing about forgiveness. It doesn't come easy. Because I wasn't sure I could ever let go of the guilt, I decided to focus on atonement. That's why," I said, turning to Mergen, "I saved you from those hockey players, why I thought to feed you. Saving you was part of my atonement." I looked away. "But that's a lie."

"No, it isn't," Mergen said, dabbing at his lips.

"Fine, but it is an incomplete truth. The whole truth, the Truth, is this: we ex-vampires lie to ourselves, saying that it was the demon inside that killed ... but when you're turned, it's not like the movies, where you lose your soul or become a mindless killer. The truth is, nothing about who you are actually changes.

"You are who you are, but with an insatiable, painful hunger that, if not satisfied, will kill you. Human blood is the only way to survive as a vampire. And your thirst for it is all-consuming. When I drank from my victims, I did so because I didn't want to die. Not because a demon was telling me to do it.

"And before you ask—pigs, cows, rats ... animal blood doesn't sustain a vampire.

"And yes, I tried to only drink the blood of those who were evil—at first. But after years of killing, even that line gets crossed. You start to find evil in all humans, no matter how small, and you lie to yourself, saying you're making the world better by ridding it of its scum. After a while, you don't even bother saying that. It just becomes a part of you. You tell yourself, you are no more evil than the man who slaughters a cow for sustenance. Being a vampire, you say, means humans have become your cattle. That is why I'm ashamed of who I was—"

"Was?" asked Mergen, clutching his stomach.

"Am ..." I said. "Am ... I am a killer who—at first—killed because I didn't want to die. And later because it just became a ... a normal thing to do."

"Mmmm," Mergen said. "The Truth may be bitter ... but it is always nourishing."

I didn't look at the avatar. I couldn't. I was so ashamed, and my eyes were so overflowing with tears that I couldn't see anything. In the clarity of my Truth, the world was a blur to see.

"Maybe," I said, "there is one more Truth to share."

Mergen's eyes glinted. "Please."

I took a deep breath. "When I turned my mother, it wasn't because I wanted to hurt or punish my father. It was because I believed that he —seeing both his daughter and wife a vampire—would agree to be turned. I wanted to have my family back. Me, mother and father, traveling the world, happy and whole. But he still refused and all I managed to do was create an immortal mother who was more trouble than a hundred angry, pitch-fork carrying, monster hunting mobs." I thought about my mother and shuddered. Just more evil I had to atone for … the stuff I did, and the insanity and chaos *she* brought into the world because of me.

I doubted I could make up for all of that even if I had a thousand lifetimes to try.

"I might have lost that round," I said, "but there was one more move I had, and on the night he …" My voice cracked, catching my next words before they could escape my lips.

"Pain is often truth newly set free," Mergen said giving me a look of divine sympathy.

I nodded, wiping away my *newly* set free tears. "So … so the night he died, was the night I took him by force and made him a vampire against his will. But my father was so stubborn. And strong. Stronger than I will ever be. As soon as he realized he could not conquer the hunger that now burned within him, he took his own life by waiting for the sun to rise. I tried to stop him, but now that he was a vampire, he was too strong for me to pull him away from the light.

" 'The sun will kill you!' I cried out.

"He just shook his head and said, 'Dying is the right thing for me to do.'

" 'But it will hurt,' I said, like a petulant child scared to take her medicine.

"He just smiled in that kind way he used to do when I was little and frightened. 'Sometimes,' he said, 'doing the right thing hurts.' And then he turned to face the dawn.

"And what did I do? I watched from the shadows as the morning light turned his body to ash."

As I sobbed in full earnest now, I realized that I wasn't crying because of the story I told. No, these tears were because I was mourning the death of my father in a way I couldn't do when I lied to myself about who I was and why I did the things I did.

A heavy hand squeezed my shoulder. Wiping away heavy tears, I saw that Mergen was trying to comfort me. But it wasn't the skinny, emaciated ghost-white man I had come to know.

He was fat. As in … Santa fat.

He drew me in close and hugged me. At first, I resisted him, but as soon as I let him hold me, and my face touched his shoulder, I wailed and lamented and howled and wept the tears of someone who had finally faced her past.

19

CHECK OUT WHAT'S BEEN CHECKED OUT

*A*fter a good, long cry, I looked up at Deirdre and Egya, who were kind enough to have walked to another side of the grove to give me my space. I stood up and, wiping away tears and runny mascara, said, "OK—it's all out of me now." I hiccupped. "Promise."

"Do you feel …" Egya paused as he searched for the word, finally settling on, "lighter?"

I didn't answer right away, taking the time to look inside myself. I felt encumbered by my tears, the heavy head that comes after a big cry. But I also felt somehow freer—like I had been wading through water and had finally gotten out of the swamp. Lighter … yes, I did feel lighter.

I nodded.

"See, milady?" He bowed. "I am Egya, here to help!"

Deirdre walked up to me and hugged me. No, it was more like she swaddled me in her big, powerful arms. "I am so glad the black man upset you and that this white man was here to comfort you," she said.

"Me, too," I chuckled. "But Deirdre, in the future it's not appropriate to—" I thought about explaining that describing humans by the color of their skin was a faux pas, but decided that was a lesson in being human that could wait for later. For now, I would try to enjoy her embrace, as tight as it was. "Oh, never mind." I hugged the changeling back.

"So," Deirdre said after she eventually let me go, "you will no longer leave?"

"Might not have a choice in the matter. We did just get run off campus. But right now I'm more concerned about avoiding roving gangs of Other-haters." I smiled grimly at the absurdity of it all. "And to think, yesterday my greatest ambition was to go to the O^3 party."

"Most certainly," Egya said. "I was going to dress as a ghost. I even bought the white sheets, complete with a pointed hood."

"Uh, Egya ... you know that costume is—"

"A joke, Darling. A joke. I may be from deepest, darkest Africa, but we still have history books."

"I don't understand," said Deirdre. "What is wrong with the black man dressing as a ghost?"

At this Egya and I laughed. Deirdre, unsure what was funny, eventually joined in, happy to see us happy. And Mergen, he seemed to be feasting from the honesty of the moment.

As our laughter died down, Deirdre said, "All I wanted to do was find my place. I am starting to think that I will not find it here."

I didn't know what to say. If *I* was struggling to find my place here, what hope did this changeling have? "Deirdre, I thought you didn't want me to leave ..."

Deirdre nodded, but it seemed she wanted to talk about something else. She pointed at the canopy of leaves around us and asked, "Will we be able to go home soon?"

"The hex should evaporate in the morning. We can go back to the dorm then and ..." I started, before I realized she wasn't talking about Gardner Hall. "Home, like ... fae? Only if the gods come back, Deirdre."

"They will never come back."

"How do you know?" I asked.

"Gods do not change their minds."

Mergen hummed in delightful agreement.

145

"And even if the hex dissipates, the humans will remember what happened this night. This will cause …" Deirdre's voice trailed as she tried to think of the right words.

"Further complications," Egya offered.

"Yes … further complications. I see little hope for us to stay."

I sighed in agreement. "Maybe. I guess we can hold out in the hope that the O³'s party will heal the divide. Justin seems to think so. But —" I shook my head "—none of this will matter if we don't find out who the killer is."

"And bring him to justice?" Deirdre asked.

"Or her," Egya pointed out.

"Justice has little to do with it. I actually think that bringing the killer in will cause more harm than good. All we do know is that an Other is doing this with magic. Bringing them to be tried under a human court's system will only focus a spotlight on the powers Others have. It will just cause more fear. I'm thinking … we should just *stop* him. Or her. As in, *permanently*."

Deirdre began stretching, as if preparing to enter a sporting competition. "Exactly, Lady Darling. Justice."

Fae logic … of course she wasn't thinking human police and court systems. Fae justice was swift and permanent—and usually justified *after* the fact.

"Justice," Egya echoed. "Justice may be blind, but I will not be so anymore. I will say what I know we have all thought. It is the Incan apu who is behind this."

I sat up so fast that my head spun. "Incan apu?"

Egya nodded. "The Other friend of the O³ Bros."

I thought of the tall, stone-skinned, sky-eyed Other. "Sal? I'd never thought that."

"Then you are a fool. Or willfully blind, like Justice."

"OK, *Egya*. Enlighten us. How can you be so sure?"

"Think about it. Dr. Dewey was part of a ritual sacrifice. Incans, Mayans, Aztec—their traditions demanded that human sacrifices be made to their gods. This is common knowledge, yes?"

Mergen smacked his lips.

"Common knowledge?" I asked. "Maybe to you. How do you know all this?

Egya shrugged. "I am a student of the dead religions—which is to say, all of them."

"Lots of religions had ritualistic sacrifices," I pointed out, having lived through many of them. "The Etruscans, the Old Chinese Dynasty, the Celts. Not just the Incans."

"True, but only one of them is enrolled in this school."

"Fine, but—"

"Just because the cave apu with baby-blue eyes smiled at you doesn't make him innocent."

"It's not that," I started, but when Mergen groaned I added, "OK—it's not *just* that. Mergen, you are really starting to annoy me."

Mergen grinned like he was just handed an ice cream cone.

I ignored the pale rider. "We can't just accuse Sal because he's *different*."

"Why not?"

"Seriously?" I said. "Ever heard of racial profiling?"

"This is different than judging someone by the color of their skin."

"How so?" I took a step toward Egya.

Deirdre, sensing my fury, stepped between us.

But Egya didn't give up. "Because a black man, Arab or Jew can't cast magic. An Incan apu can."

I shook my head. "I refuse to blindly accuse him—"

"The jinni guard dog and the hex required magic, Kat. Any Other is a suspect. But the sacrifice—that is part of the Incan mythos. Put two and two together and you get ..." He made a fist.

"Yes, but—"

"But nothing. You know I'm right. You must." He looked at Mergen for confirmation, but, much to his (and my) surprise, Mergen neither smacked his lips nor groaned in disgust.

"See?" I said, as if this proved anything.

"See what? His complete lack of reaction makes my words neither true nor false. It just means that you're still being willfully blind."

"Oh, you self-righteous—"

"What?" he said.

"Stupid little …"

"What else?"

"Know-it-all!" I yelled. Not my best insult. And in utter fury, I turned around and kicked the mesh fence that surrounded the base of the cross. I guess no one really ever cleaned the thing, because a cloud of dust flew up into the air, creating neon rays of light.

Now here I was literally basking in the cross's rays. That's when I realized how stupid I was being.

"Deirdre," I said, pointing up at the neon icon, "what did you call that thing earlier?"

"The cross? A symbol that offers protection for those who wish it to."

"Exactly … a symbol that offers *protection* for those who wish it to. Or maybe, for those *it wishes to*. It all makes sense now!"

"What makes sense now?" Egya asked, cocking his head to one side in confusion.

"Sneak me back onto campus."

"Why?"

"To confirm something."

"Confirm what?"

"Who the killer is."

"Confirm *what*, girl?" Egya said. "We *know* who the killer is."

"Maybe," I conceded. "But I have a theory that might prove otherwise. You may be right about the apu, but I think there may be more to it than that. Come down with me, help me break into the library, and keep an open mind. If I'm wrong, I will hunt the apu down with you. But if I'm right, we will have saved an innocent Other from … well … us. Agreed?" I stuck out my hand.

Egya looked at it for a long moment. "If your theory proves false, we go after the apu without hesitation?"

"Without hesitation."

Egya took my hand and let out an unnatural cackle.

I guess he still had a bit of hyena in him, after all.

* * *

We waited until the dead of night to sneak back onto campus. By that time, the place was deserted, but the remnants of the vigil remained. Flowers, unlit candles, homemade signs ... the relics of a human farewell.

As we made our way up the steps and into the Other Studies Library, we passed the Old Librarian's picture, and I felt as though his eyes were watching me.

Police tape still hung over the entrance, creating a barrier that was more psychological than physical. I hesitated at the yellow ribbons, but Deirdre, who did not share my cultural apprehension for the invisible barrier of authority (and who also had a great disdain toward plastic), just ripped through it and into the library.

I followed the changeling inside, praying to the GoneGods that Egya had been successful in disabling the alarm. It wouldn't stop the cameras from recording our entrance, but given that we were all wearing wide hats Deirdre had fashioned from leaves and foliage, I doubted we'd be recognized. Once inside, I made my way to the display where the Old Librarian had been strung up. We skirted the smashed shelves and torn books still littering the expanse of the library floor. I guess with Dr. Dewey gone, there was no one to clean this mess up. At least his body was still gone ... and the CSI's cleanup crew had mopped up the blood and any other body parts that might be considered a biohazard.

At the display case, the main part of the crime scene, little plastic tents with numbers on them littered the floor. Most of them stood next to items used in the ritual: a scalpel, three buckets holding red-stained towels (I guess the killer wanted to control the blood flow), a few vases and other decorative items that prettied up the murder. Rituals are nothing without their shrouds, vases and incense, right?

Several placeholders stood where the jars or containers with bits of body in them had been. They had been taken away as either evidence or part of the bio cleanup. I tried to remember what was next to the lone placeholders before going over to the display and looking for the one clue I needed to confirm my theory. Walking among the ransacked display cases, I didn't have to look into more than a couple of them before I found what I was looking for. Well, several *whats* I was looking for.

"I knew it," I said.

"Knew what?" Egya said, emerging from the shadows. He held up several wires in his hands. "Disabled alarm. Elegant solution."

"The obsidian knife," I said. "It isn't here."

"So?"

"Obsidian knives are central to Mayan and Aztec ritual sacrifices— not Incan, like you'd said. The obsidian knife is missing, but not the Feast Bowl. Why would an Incan apu go to all the trouble to steal the blade, but not the other ritualistic items? It doesn't make sense."

"Again, so?" Egya said.

"So—look at what *is* missing."

I walked over to a smashed display case and pulled out the little card bearing the description, handing it to the former were-hyena. He read it. "GoneGodsDamn it! I'm going to kill them all," he growled.

"I'm sure you will," I said. "And I'll be right there with you."

Mergen, hearing his unbridled rage, belched. He made a gesture that indicated he couldn't possibly eat another bite.

20

LET'S PARTY LIKE IT'S YOUR LAST
DAY ON EARTH

(Except It's Not and the World Already Ended)

*T*he party started, not with a bang but, rather, a parade.

I had heard the university parties were a big deal, but this was something else.

The O³ Bros had arranged that some of the more enthusiastic participants would parade up the hill together. Hundreds of kids—all dressed up as minotaurs, valkyrie, angels, wendigos, kappas, cyclopes, elves and a whole host of Others I didn't recognize—made a slow ascent up the hill toward the area that stood between the four dorms. McConnell, Molson and Gardner Hall served as a net, bordering the three sides of an uneven field all the dorms shared. In the center of the field stood an old, circular building that housed the mess hall, a large open courtyard at its center. In the center of this courtyard was an old stone fountain that hadn't worked in years.

Slowly, deliberately, the partiers poured into the courtyard, Others dressed as humans and humans dressed as Others. Some of the humans were so well-disguised that I mistook them for Others, and only after a double take—sometimes a triple take—did I recognize them as human. And not from a flaw in their costume. It was their mannerisms that gave them away: an oversized dwarf running his hands through his hair in a very nervous, human way; a tiny minotaur chugging a beer; an overaccessorized valkyrie vaping.

And then there were the misinformed humans. The ones with fake vampire fangs or those prancing around in werewolf costumes. They clearly hadn't gotten the memo that those once-upon-a-time kinds of monsters no longer existed.

Not that it mattered. In a way, I was comforted that vampires and werewolves were still something humans thought about (huh, *humans* —look at me refer to them like I wasn't one myself).

I walked through the crowd of humans pretending to be Others, when some shirtless boy shoved a plastic cup filled with beer at me and said, "Nice sword. What are you supposed to be? A Scottish baby?" He chuckled at his oh-so-funny joke. His trousers were furry and his feet looked hooved. A satyr. He even held a pan flute in one of his hands—nice touch. With that beer in his other hand and that wicked grin, he could have been Pan himself.

I was wearing my father's mask and my old Stewart tartan, which was older than this guy's grandfather. Still, he was acting in good humor, and this was a party, after all. I curtsied—not an easy feat when you have a dirk wrapped around your waist—and in my poshest British accent I said, "A Cherub warrior, actually. And before you ask, yes, all angels are from Scotland."

At this, he guffawed and handed me five tickets that reminded me of the coupons you won at a carnival. "You're a funny gal. Here—beer tickets. Enjoy." And with that, he pranced off with such grace that for a moment I thought he might actually be Pan.

I looked at the tickets I held and shrugged. "When in Rome," I muttered to myself, and made my way to the makeshift bar the O^3 Bros had set up beside the fountain.

* * *

As I approached the beer stand, I scanned the crowd. After what I'd seen—or rather, *didn't* see—in the library, I was pretty sure the killer would use the chaos of this party to enact the next phase of his plan.

Or *her* plan. I still wasn't certain about that.

There were so many people, though, all dressed up in so many disguises, that I wasn't sure how I'd ever find him. Luckily I wasn't alone. Deirdre was somewhere in this crowd, dressed like a purple ninja—the only costume that covered her face we could come up with, given our limited wardrobe. Egya wore an uninspired white sheet with eyes cut out—his version of a ghost. I guess he wasn't kidding about the costume, after all. And without the hood, he thankfully just looked like a kid under a sheet. As for Mergen—well, that guy had eaten so much Truth on the mountain that he'd literally swelled up to the size of a plump fat man.

So we dressed him like Santa Claus.

All we had to do was find the killer. Trouble was, based on our investigations, the killer was *human*, not an Other like the hex had led us to believe. You see—and this was where I was particularly proud of my Nancy Drew skills—I noticed that the only items used in the killing ritual and the only items stolen from the library were *human* relics used in *human* sacrifice. Ancient rope, a ceremonial bowl and the obsidian dagger.

Others—particularly the human-sacrificing kind—didn't use such items. By their logic, there was too much distance between the human and victim when using a crucifix: better to bind them with magic. Granted, magic was in limited supply these days, but still, they wouldn't crucify their victims. Why use a Christian symbol to taint their own traditions, when simply tying them to a chair was enough?

And as for the ceremonial bowl—why use something as silly as a bowl when it was much better to drink the blood straight from the source? I should know—ex-vampire here, remember?

An obsidian blade looks cool, sure, but claws are much easier to use.

All that told me was the killer had never been an Other. But what it didn't explain was the jinni guard dog that attacked us in the library, or the hex cast on me afterward. A human cannot conjure something like that, and so it really created a huge plot hole for us. Until, that is—and this was the pièce de résistance—we found one of Solomon's rings shattered in its case.

Even though it's in the Bible, few people understand what King Solomon's rings were about. Solomon was the "wise king," the guy who could supposedly speak to the "other world." All that was true, but it was the nature of *how* it was true that few understand. King Solomon could capture and control jinn. As in, otherworldly creatures that God made from smokeless fire.

What a power.

Only problem with his power was that he had to capture the jinn in gems. Gems that he fashioned into rings, bracelets, belts ... you name it.

Seems the Other Studies Library had inherited a boatload of them.

Few people would know that ... *could* know that. But an Occultist bastard hell-bent on performing human sacrifice might. Knowing the power of the ring and being backed into a corner—the corner of being caught by a certain ex-vampire girl wandering into the library in the middle of the night—would have been motivation enough to release the jinni from its eternal prison. Luckily for us, the killer must have returned to the scene of the crime sometime after I'd been hauled off to the police station and returned the ring to its case. Must have thought the police would just assume it had been broken in the debacle along with so many other things and wouldn't put two and two together. Too bad for the killer—I'd had the last three hundred years to bone up on my history and lore. The instant I saw the broken ring, I knew the answer.

And as for the hex? That was witches' magic. Witches, just like vampires and werewolves, lost their magic when the gods left. But they didn't lose their talismans. It was perfectly conceivable that a witch might have imbued an item in her possession with a hexing spell. In fact, it was perfectly conceivable that she might have dozens of items, all imbued with various nasty, onetime spells at her disposal.

And so, all these facts led us to the same conclusion—the killer was human.

And, most likely, at this party.

Trouble was, there was an overwhelming number of humans at this party. Talk about finding a body in a mass grave (sorry, sick vampire humor).

The line to the bar was moving at a snail's pace; given that it literally wove around the entire courtyard, I'd be here for a while. But standing in a line was as good a vantage point as any from which to look for the killer. Looking up and down the line, I saw the last person I wanted to see standing right in front of me.

The mousey girl who got that poor gargoyle killed.

* * *

I took a double take, but there was no mistaking her. There she was, dressed in a catsuit complete with fake cat ears pinned to her hair and a silly cat's tail pinned to her arse. Ironic that someone so mousey would dress as a cat, but hey, I guess we all aspire to be something we're not from time to time.

I knew that I had something really important to do. I knew that confronting her would be the worst thing I could do at this moment. But I also knew that I might never have another chance to tell that bitch what a horrible thing she had done. There would be no justice for that unfortunate gargoyle, but there might be a little retribution.

I leaned forward and pulled at her cat's tail. She whirled around, and her stupid mascara whiskers were in my face. Our eyes connected, and I saw the regular fear and anxiety constantly on her face. She didn't know who I was—as far as she could tell, I was some drunk cherub having a bit of fun. She tried to smile, but given how nervous she was, all she managed to pull off was a troubled smirk. I now saw that it took every ounce of her nervous, anxiety-ridden being to dress up and come to this party.

Not that I cared.

"You," I said, dropping my posh British accent, "have been a very naughty girl."

"I have?" she said.

I lifted my cherub mask for a second before lowering it again.

Her eyes flashed with recognition.

"You abandoned someone who only wanted to fit in—just like you," I said. "What's more, you abandoned someone who would have protected you. I would have thought someone as weak and pathetic as you would have—"

"Georgie," she said, scanning the crowd. "Is he here?"

I paused. "Georgie?"

"Yeah," she said, leaning in close. "The gargoyle. Is he here?"

They must have gotten a few extra hands at the bar. The line started moving, and within seconds we were making a slow march toward drinks. "You mean you didn't ..."

I suddenly realized I had automatically assumed she was responsible for the gargoyle's death. But in reality, I didn't know. "No ... Georgie isn't here. What happened yesterday?"

We were walking side by side now, and I was starting to feel like a real moron.

"We were walking home," she said, "talking. He was telling me all about his role in protecting some medieval king. Chlo-something."

"Chlothar the Great," I corrected her. "It was from the Gargouille where all gargoyles were born from. They rose when Chlothar was king."

"Yeah, that's it. We had a good time, and we decided we'd go up to the gazebo. You know, the one on the hill behind the dorms. We cut through the stadium's parking lot. It was the middle of the afternoon, so we figured it was safe enough. And when we got in, we saw several hockey players loading their gear into the van, laughing and having fun. You know, boys being boys."

"And what? They saw Georgie and attacked him?"

She shook her head. "Not at all. They didn't even look in our direction. Not until ..." She stopped talking and her shoulders scrunched up like she was literally trying to make herself smaller. Even in a cat costume, she managed to look like a mouse.

"Until what?" I asked.

"This woman stepped out of a car. She walked over to the passenger side and opened the door. A boy our age stepped out. But she wasn't looking at him. Her eyes were fixed on Georgie. She had a wicked smile on her face, and as we walked past she pointed at Georgie and said, 'How convenient.' Then ... then she *slapped* the boy. Georgie didn't like that. Not one bit."

"You mean some kid was being slapped by his mother?"

She shook her head. "No. First of all, the boy's a student here. I've seen him around. And as for the woman—she was too young to be his mother. But she was mad. And she slapped him *hard*. Weird thing was, she wasn't looking at him when she hit him. She was looking at *us*. Well, not us—at Georgie. 'Let's see if this works,' she said. Her voice was eerie, like she was trying out something she shouldn't. Then she slapped the boy again. And again. That's when Georgie started shaking his head and huffing. Then that crazy woman pulled out a gun and pointed it at the boy's head. That's when Georgie started to *really* get mad, but the woman didn't seem worried. She just pointed at the group of hockey players who were no longer loading their gear into the van, but were now staring at her. 'If you want him to live,' she said to Georgie, 'then you'll take care of them.' He looked at me and said, 'Run. Please. I'll find you later, but you must run now. Run, run, run!' The woman giggled at this and pulled back the hammer on her pistol. That's when Georgie's eyes turned red and he charged at the group of hockey players. I mean, he was like a creature possessed. But that wasn't him. He wouldn't just attack them and—and ..." She trailed off.

"What happened after that? What did you do?"

She looked around before lowering her head in shame. "What do you think I did? I ran, just like he told me to." She shook her head and dabbed the corners of her eyes with the end of her tail. "I shouldn't have left. But I was so scared. And he was so angry." Then she clamped her fists at her sides and her voice took on a bit more confidence. "But that's why I'm here now. I'm looking for Georgie. He's going to live with me...just like you and—"

Mousey Girl so abruptly stopped walking that the people directly behind us bumped into her back. Not that she noticed. She just pointed in front of her and said, "That's the woman who made Georgie so crazy."

21

SCREAMING THE GODS BACK

I looked up to see where Mousey Girl was pointing, half expecting to see some crazed Occultist standing with the obsidian blade in one hand and a rain stick in the other. What I didn't expect to see was Detective Wilcox, standing next to Nate.

They stood on the far side of the fountain, too far to discern any real detail, but close enough for me to clearly make out who they were. If I could recognize them, that meant they could recognize me. For a split second, my heart started to race. Either Mousey Girl had gotten all her facts wrong or Detective Wilcox was somehow involved in all this. Which meant she was probably responsible for the hex. My heart skipped a beat—until I remembered I was wearing the cherub's mask.

I breathed a sigh of relief, then scanned the crowd for Mergen, Deirdre or Egya. None of them were in sight. The only familiar face—other than Wilcox and Nate—was the apu, Sal, standing by himself and looking pretty glum. And since Wilcox was with Nate, one of the apu's closest friends, I couldn't be sure which side he was on. Damn it!

Mousey Girl turned to run away. I grabbed her arm and said, "Where are you going?"

"Away," she whispered in a rushed voice.

I looked up at Wilcox, who seemed to be scanning the crowd, looking for someone. Nate, on the other hand, looked dejected, frustrated and scared.

But Mousey Girl could easily get away. From where we stood, she could veer to the right and use the beer line as cover. Even if Wilcox recognized her as the girl in the parking lot, Mousey Girl would be long gone before anything could happen.

"OK," I said. "Go—but before you do, I have a question. Do you know the gargoyle's real name?"

"Huh?" she said, fear filling her mascara-decorated eyes.

"The gargoyle. Georgie. Do you know his real name? We want to give him a proper burial and, well, his name will go a long way toward making that happen."

I don't know if she even heard my question, or else she'd probably have started bawling from the discovery that her new friend was dead. But her eyes were trained on Wilcox. The line edged forward. Mousey Girl's terror quickly got the best of her. She pulled her arm away and disappeared into the crowd.

I was alone in the line. At least I wouldn't be recognized, which meant I could get close enough to confirm or deny Mousey Girl's story without being detected. The line edged forward until we were almost parallel with Wilcox, with the fountain between us. As I got close enough to make out some details, I realized that Mousey Girl had only been half-right.

Detective Wilcox wasn't just the terrifying lady who'd gotten Georgie the gargoyle killed.

She was the crazy woman who was going to get everyone at this party slaughtered.

* * *

The line was meandering along, snaking around the courtyard, closer and closer to where Wilcox was standing, and now that she was only yards away, I could see she hadn't had only the one Solomon's ring, used and abandoned at the library—she had dozens. The sharp ruby-red diamonds lined each of her ten fingers, most sporting two rings each, and at least a dozen more hung from her belt as seemingly harmless decoration. And that's exactly why I hadn't seen her wearing any yesterday. She knew she could get away with displaying them in the open at a GoneGodsDamned costume party.

The most frightening thing about her was how she wore the rings. The glass parts were facing inward, which meant that all she needed to do was clap her hands together and she'd shatter all the rings at once. Not that she was poised to do that now, thank the GoneGods. She had one arm around Nate and the other in her jacket like she was holding—

They were standing next to the dried-up stone fountain, and now I noticed for the first time that something was different about the fountain than the last time I'd been here: it was decorated with vines and orchids and lilies and several other plants, and its stone, bench-like edge had been cleared as if as a table or ... a botanical tabernacle. The perfect surface to perform a ritual on—and I knew exactly what kind of ritual she had in mind.

We advanced a few steps in the queue. As I drew nearer, one detail became clearer—she was holding a gun on Nate. Looking behind me at Sal, I suddenly realized why he was so distraught. He knew Detective Wilcox was threatening his friend. As an apu, he was bound to protect his friends in a way that went beyond fraternal loyalty. He was created to protect those in his charge. That was his purpose for being ... and right now he was helpless to protect his friend.

The rings, the trapped jinn, Dr. Dewey's murder, threatening Nate —it was all starting to make sense. But there were still some missing pieces. Missing pieces I didn't have time to contemplate now.

Because now I needed to stop Wilcox from going through with whatever plan she had in mind.

I left the queue and walked toward the fountain, swaying like I was just another drunk reveler, until I was standing right next to Wilcox.

Then, using a handy wrist move I'd learned from an aikido master in Japan, I forced her to release the gun and pulled her hand out of her jacket, while simultaneously lacing my fingers with hers. She tried to punch me with her free hand, no longer holding Nate. I rolled into the punch so as to weaken the impact enough that none of the rings would shatter against the hard surface of my mask.

No jinn appeared. My move had worked. I breathed a sigh of relief, then kicked her in the shins and laced my other hand with hers. Now we were hand-in-hand-in-hand-in-hand.

She tried to pull away and I just went with it. I might not be able to match her strength—after all, she had three inches on me—but that didn't mean I couldn't inconvenience her. And as long as my fingers were laced with hers, she couldn't break the glass and release the jinn.

"What are you doing?" she yelled.

People were starting to gather around us, evidently getting into position to watch a catfight. Well, a cherub-versus-gypsy fight. That was fine. I didn't mind an audience.

"Nate," I said. "Run." The way I figured it, as long as Nate was safe, Sal would be able to help. As it was, Sal was walking toward us, trying to determine if Nate was, indeed, far enough away for him to get involved.

But Nate didn't move.

"Come on—run! Sal and I can take care of her."

Wilcox and I turned in a tight circle as she tried to pull free, so Nate was now behind me. Therefore, I could only imagine that his face transformed from fear to malice the second before I heard him say, "Why would I want to do that?"

Then I felt a heavy hand grab my shoulder and pull.

* * *

GoneGodsDamn it! Nate was actually trying to help Wilcox. I'd read this situation oh, so wrong.

"What the hell are you doing?" I cried out.

162

He leaned in and whispered, "What do you think? We're trying to get them back."

"Them?"

"The gods ... we disappointed them when we turned our backs on the old ways." I could feel his hot breath on me. "And now we have the ability to do it. Finally."

"How?" I asked, as the three of us swayed in a weird dance. I wasn't about to let go of Wilcox's hands, and moving so the rings stayed intact while shrugging off Nate as he tried to pull me off her was no easy feat. It meant going with the flow, with both of them. Trouble was, they had opposite flows, and the only thing that prevented them from breaking free was that they had yet to coordinate their efforts.

"Idiot," Wilcox hissed. "The apu is bound to protect Nate. And by threatening him, I am forcing the apu to do as I demand."

Oops. That should have been obvious. "And what's that?"

Kind of wished I hadn't asked, because her eyes widened with anticipation and excitement. And not in an *I just won the lottery* kind of way. It was more like after a lifetime of being a vegetarian, I'd just had my first steak and now that I knew the taste of flesh, I'd never go back. My similes needed work, I know, but I was under a pinch of duress at the time.

"The gods," Wilcox practically moaned, "they left because we turned our backs on them. We no longer honored them the way they wanted. We no longer paid them tribute. I am here to usher back the old ways."

"And by 'old ways,' which ones are you talking about?"

"Blood tributes," Wilcox said.

"You mean human sacrifice?"

"Is there any other kind?" Nate asked as he pulled.

We continued our dance, and all the while I saw the confusion on Sal's face. He couldn't hear our conversation or assess the level of threat against Nate. All he could do was helplessly watch as he waited for some clear indication of what to do.

"So it was Nate at the library?" I said. "You didn't release the jinni from the ring—you don't have the power. But the guard dog is a protective creature, and it released itself because Nate was threatened."

"That's what's amazing about the apu's power. He uses what is around him to protect his charges. In the library, that meant breaking the ring. At the vigil, when you so conveniently threatened Nate, Sal's protection took the form of a hex that literally turned these otherwise reasonable human beings into a roving gang of hate."

Mousey Girl's story suddenly made sense. A gargoyle's nature is to protect their charge. When Detective Wilcox threatened Nate in front of him, not only was his commitment to Mousey Girl's safety being tested, but he was also falling under the Incan Other's spell; the two opposite forces were being pitted against each other, and Sal's spell won. Georgie attacked those hockey players because, at that moment, it was literally the only thing Sal could do to stop Wilcox from hurting Nate.

"The apu's spell contains so much beauty in its simplicity," Wilcox said. "And since I am a constant threat to Nate, there is only one solution for the apu."

"Do your bidding?"

"Do my bidding," she repeated, her eyes widening again in a maniacal expression. "And my bidding is to sacrifice all these silly kids just like they did when the sun would turn black in displeasure and demand human blood as a tribute. The apu was hesitant but not as hesitant as you would expect. After all, he is a creature who was once given human tributes himself."

"But you're not really threatening Nate, so why would he—"

At this, Wilcox made a mock pouting expression. "You mean, would I kill my little cousin? Without hesitation."

"Thanks, dear cuz," Nate said with venom in his own voice.

"So the solution is simple," I said. "Remove you, remove the threat."

That's when the worst thing happened.

From behind me I felt a powerful force rip Nate off of me. I turned just in time to see Deirdre standing over Nate, her broadsword raised over her head.

"You dare harm milady?!" she cried out.

"No, Deirdre—don't!"

But my words were drowned out by the sound of a glass-shattering noise.

Wilcox's rings were all broken, releasing an army of angry, over-protective jinn onto the party.

22

CHANGELINGS, HYENAS, WARRIORS AND ANGELS

What happened next was nothing short of awe-inspiring, chaotic and terrifying. Thirty-one jinn burst out of Wilcox's hands and belt. Thirty-one creatures—and not all of them were guard dogs like those from the library. There were all types: a monkey-looking creature the size of a wendigo, a monster with a human head on a body the shape of a horse-sized chicken, a ten-foot-long ferret with a scorpion's tail. Hell, I even saw a couple salmon bigger than park benches swimming through the air.

Thirty-one creatures of all shapes and sizes. Thirty-one creatures, each possessing immense power. Thirty-one creatures, all hell-bent on doing one thing.

Protecting Nate.

* * *

I expected the jinn to just go on an all-out rampage, but they didn't. Instead, they hovered (well, those that could hover; others leered, crouched or just stood vigilantly, dozens of tiny eyes staring in every which direction) around Nate and Wilcox, employing the dead fountain as an ad hoc base of operations.

Legend said that whoever wore the broken crystal controlled the jinn. But Wilcox didn't have the power to actually *release* the jinn. That was Sal. His protective magic would have forced them out in order to protect Nate. Nevertheless, now that they were released, they were under Wilcox's control ... and as long as her commands didn't threaten Nate, they would do her bidding.

Wilcox looked around, turned to me and said, "This wasn't how I imagined this going down."

I lifted an eyebrow beneath my cherub mask and scanned the crowd behind me. All eyes were on us—not surprising, given that thirty-one creatures had suddenly appeared out of thin air, and we were apparently the source. Deirdre was behind me in her ninja costume, her broadsword at the ready, but she was smart enough to bide her time and wait for an opening. The only eyes that didn't seem to be on us were those of Egya and Mergen, who were nowhere in sight. I could only hope they were up to something useful.

"I was going for more gravitas," Wilcox explained. "Ah well, too late now." Fishing around in her jacket, she pulled out the obsidian blade and pointed it at the crowd. Speaking to her guard creatures, she said, "Make sure nobody escapes."

Jinn went every which way, and the screams and panic began in earnest. I heard the loudest shouts of alarm toward the edges of the courtyard, which surprised me. I looked up and saw that someone had slid thick mesh fences across all the exits leading into the surrounding building. No escaping the mess hall, apparently. I don't even know how they'd managed to install sliding cage doors like that without anyone noticing. These guys were good.

Then Wilcox pointed at the cleared-off altar on the fountain and said, "Bring me the virgin."

A nasnas (a creature that looked like a man cut in half from navel to forehead) hopped through the crowd and picked up a large shirtless boy dressed like a Roman legioneer. "Hey," the boy cried out. "I'm not a virgin! I've done it. Lots."

Oh, brother. If it wasn't so horrible, it would have been funny. But as it stood, seeing the terror in that kid's eyes, there was nothing *ha-ha* about this moment.

I turned to Nate. "Come on, Nate—this won't bring the gods back. This can't."

"You … you don't know that."

"Indeed," Wilcox said with a laugh. "No one does. We'll just have to try and then wait and see."

The nasnas placed the large "virgin" on the tabernacle, and Wilcox commanded it to tie him up, handing the nasnas an ancient rope. As he was being strapped to the stone, Wilcox teased her sacrifice-to-be with the obsidian blade.

Turning to the crowd, she cried out, "I know what many of you are thinking. How do I know something that so many scholars, philosophers, scientists, politicians and theologians don't know? The answer is simple—they know, too. They just don't have the balls to say it: the gods left because we disappointed them."

Then she began chanting. One hand on the blade, which she slowly raised above her head. The other on her gun.

"Nate," I heard a voice say behind me. "Are you doing this?" Justin approached me from behind, perfectly intact, not a single jinni attacking him. And then it hit me that none of Nate's circle of friends would be harmed, just as had been the case with the hex. The apu's spell wouldn't allow it. Five fewer people to worry about.

Justin walked past me, panting heavily. He had obviously been running. "Tell me she's not telling the truth, Nate. Tell me you have nothing to do with this."

Nate didn't move as Wilcox continued her chant. Justin took another step forward, but two jinn—one resembling Swamp Thing, the other an actual dinosaur—positioned themselves so that he couldn't proceed. They didn't attack him, mind you, but they didn't let him through, either.

"Come on," he said, "we can't let her do this. This isn't right. This isn't *right!*"

But Nate's expression stayed the same. He didn't move. Nothing changed.

Justin wiped away a tear from frustration. "Why is this happening?"

"Because of me," Sal said, his hollow voice somehow piercing the screams of all those being corraled by the jinn like cattle.

Justin gave him a curious look. "You?"

Sal nodded. "My spell. These creatures emerged because Nate was threatened. And she possesses the rings." He pointed at Wilcox, who laughed in agreement. "As long as she does, they will obey her."

"Then ... turn it off," Justin said.

"I ... I can't. I am an apu. My magic demands that I protect those I love."

"And do you not love *them*?" Justin said, gesturing to the roiling crowd all around them.

Sal looked around and shook his head. "I tried, but none of them have accepted me. Not like you and Nate. They give me strange looks and speak to me with trembling voices. They're afraid of me, and because of that fear, they keep their distance." Sal's eyes turned from their usual crisp sky-blue to a stormy gray.

"And *this* will make that better?" Justin shook his head. "This isn't right, Sal. If you can't love them, then at least feel *empathy* for them. Protect *them*, too."

I could see what Justin was doing—he was trying to get the apu to extend his protection spell. For a moment I thought it just might work, but then Sal shook his head, a cloudy tear falling from his face. "I can't. I'm sorry."

"Fine," Justin said. Showing exactly why he was the star of the football team, he faked past the two jinn and ran up to Nate. "If you can't protect everyone, maybe you can find it in your heart to choose."

Then Justin did something I will admire for the rest of my life. Knowing full well what would happen, he walked right up to Nate and punched him.

Right in the nose.

"Man, what I wouldn't give to be the one to punch that kid in the nose."

Deirdre glanced over at me, arching one eyebrow.

"What?" I said. "It's the Truth."

Where was Mergen when I needed him?

* * *

Nate fell down as if in slow motion, and before his butt could hit the ground with a thump, I heard a sound that could only be described as rolling thunder ... rolling closer and closer to us.

"Shit!" I yelled out. "Justin!"

In one fluid motion, I slid between the dinosaur jinni's legs and tackled Justin, pushing him behind me just as a dozen jinn turned on him, seeking to protect Nate. "Get behind me!" I pulled out my dirk and waited.

The jinn charged forward.

They would have to get through me first if they wanted Justin.

There were far too many for one ex-vampire, of course, but I figured I could cut down a few of them before they'd get by. At that moment, Deirdre appeared at my side and I realized that we might be able to dispatch more than a few before they eventually overcame us.

As far as last stands, this wasn't the worst way to go.

I readied myself, gritting my teeth behind my mask, just as my father might have once done.

But the jinn didn't attack.

Instead, they hovered about in confusion, staring at both Justin and Nate.

The jinn had been paralyzed by indecision.

Seems the apu wouldn't let them hurt *anyone* in his charge ... and this was something he took very seriously. Even knowing his friend had used him and recognizing the pain and suffering this had caused, he still could not let harm fall upon him. Say what you will about Sal —once he was your friend, he was your friend for life.

But at least the jinn weren't attacking anyone. Thank the Gone-Gods for small miracles.

Justin, standing behind us, cried out, "Come on. You coward! Come *on!*" But he didn't try to get at Nate again.

"Nate," I called over my shoulder, still facing the confused jinn.

"You know this isn't right. All you have to do is say one word and this can all stop."

Wilcox's chanting got louder as the obsidian blade rose higher in her fist. She was going to kill that poor kid any second now, and I was stuck on the far side of the fountain, surrounded by monstrous jinn, powerless to stop her.

I might have been powerless ... but the *Truth* wasn't.

Without warning, a hail of arrows flew at Wilcox. I turned to see Mergen lumbering into view at a speed that shouldn't be possible for someone so fat. His bow was out and he was shooting arrows with a velocity and accuracy that wasn't only divine in nature—it was also badass.

Mergen must have been seven feet tall now, and just as wide, his Santa costume ripping at the seams. He looked like a Jolly Ol' Nick version of the Incredible Hulk. I guess the Truth of everyone's terror became an all-you-can-eat foie gras–style buffet for him, literally funneling nourishment into his being. He grew with every cry, every scream, and his size and speed made him the most formidable warrior on the field.

But as accurate and fast as his arrows were, the jinn were faster. They caught every arrow before any could hit Wilcox. Not that this deterred Mergen any. He just kept them coming.

A thought occurred to me. Every single jinn was occupied stopping his typhoon of arrows.

A diversion. Hell yeah, Mergen!

I jumped up onto the fountain, skirting all the decorations and the jinn toward the side with the tabernacle. Slicing off the tail of the ferret-scorpion jinni, I jumped on the poor sacrificial legioneer and struck at Wilcox. The ferret-scorpion tried to grab me with its paws, but it was too late. I was already up in the air again. But before I could make contact with Wilcox, two jinn zipped up between us, protecting her from mortal danger.

Mortal danger—but not pain. I brought down my dirk on the only exposed part of her—the hand that held the obsidian blade.

I missed. Sort of. I had been aiming to cut her hand clear off, but because of the angle, all I managed to do was cut through her thumb, the hilt of her dagger stopping my sword from making a clean cut.

Still, I severed her thumb. Anyone who has ever operated an sacrifical alter will tell you that you need a thumb to sacrifice a human.

Wilcox cried out in pain just as three jinn came on me. I was sure it was only a matter of seconds before they disemboweled me for my little maneuver, but instead, they softened my fall, gently putting me on the floor.

"What the—?" I started.

"You are willing to die to protect them," I heard a voice echo.

I looked up to see the apu crying tears of confusion. He knelt down over me, sending a shifting dust of stone around us.

"Yes ...?" I said.

"Then you are the real protector of this realm. Not I," he said, and his impossible sky-blue eyes became gray and sullen, matching his stony skin. "I surrender this place to you."

"No more spell?" I said.

"No more spell," said the apu, lowering his head.

"No more spell? You idiots!" Wilcox said, grabbing her bleeding hand. "You served your purpose. The jinn are free from their bounds of protection, and still under my control."

"Not all of them," Egya said.

In all the confusion, I didn't see him sneaking up behind her. Egya wasn't only silent, he was practically invisible—I had no idea how he had got past all those jinn defenses. Until it hit me: he'd approached without the intention of hurting Wilcox, the jinn's new sole master. He was just some silent kid moving in this direction—that raised no alarms, didn't set off any defenses. His willpower to control his thoughts was incredible. How could he be so disciplined?

I could learn a lot from that kid.

He no longer wore his ridiculous ghost costume, but instead was shirtless, a Ngbaka throwing knife at his waist. He held a Ngombe sword in one hand, its looping tips looking like the scythe's evil twin, and his other hand was aloft, holding something that glinted in the light.

Then I realized what he was up to. He held Wilcox's thumb in his hand, the crystal ring still on the flesh. Pulling it off and letting the thumb drop to the courtyard floor, he gracefully slid the ring onto his own finger and said in a tone far too casual for such an awesome move, "Jinn—bring me her belt."

In a whirl, a giant hawk circled Wilcox and, faster than you could say, *Holy sh—*, the belt was in Egya's hand.

Wilcox knew she was done. There was only one move left for her to do, and the bitch did it. Raising her nine fingers with seventeen rings, she cried out, *"Kill them! Kill them all!"*

* * *

That set them off. Oh, GoneGods, did it ever.

Jinn went every which way at once—lunging on humans as they did. I watched in horror as teeth and claws and talons (and scales, in the case of the giant salmon) lashed out at the totally shocked humans, and that's when I realized there was no way to get out of this without casualties. Wilcox may only have had control of half the jinn, but that was still enough to cause mayhem and confusion.

The monkey jinni lunged at two kids who were dressed like dark elves (but then again, they might have just been dressed goth). I leapt up and stabbed the creature in the back. It writhed in pain and turned to face me, twisting its long, skeletal talon to strike my face. But I was ready for that. Ducking under its swing, I took advantage of its momentum to thrust my dirk into its neck.

It squirmed and tried to screech, but its cries of agony only forced fire-yellow blood out of its neck wound faster.

I managed to pull my dirk from its corpse and stay relatively unscathed.

One down—sixteen to go.

In the carnage, I saw Deirdre swinging her broadsword in defense as she ushered students across the courtyard. She wasn't trying to kill any of the jinn, but rather place herself between them and the students. I suppose you could say she had pledged her sword arm to the entire student body. A student body that had been less than kind to her and all Others. In that moment, I felt a surge of pride for my fae roommate.

I also caught a glimpse of Egya. He was commanding the jinn under his control to protect the innocent. He, too, wasn't going for the kill, using his long arms and powerful swing to protect those who were trying to run.

Mergen continued his barrage of arrows at Wilcox, filling the three jinn protecting her like pincushions.

But the three of them could only cover so much. This wasn't going to go well, unless—

As I watched Mergen shoot another arrow, which lodged itself in the tiny forearm of the Tyrannosaurus rex, I saw Wilcox pull Nate away, through the crazed crowd, flanked all the while by a swimming salmon. As she reached a far exit, the mesh door slid open just long enough for her to yank Nate through before slamming shut again.

She was taking him to McConnell Hall.

Evidently, she thought she'd watch the chaos unfold from the relative safety inside.

* * *

Remember how I'd said that, while certain ex-Others had lost their *magical* abilities, they still retained a certain amount of latent skill? Sure, I didn't have a taste for blood anymore, but I'd always be a master at kung fu. Witches lost their powers to cast spells, but they could still use talismans they'd already imbued with magic. Werehyenas ... well, I wasn't quite sure *what* Egya could do.

Point is, I was determined to follow Wilcox and Nate, and a simple caged door wasn't going to stop me. A couple hundred years ago, I'd developed a pretty kickass ability to scale the wall of just about any building. Castles were my specialty. So this courtyard's perimeter walls weren't going to pose any challenge.

I left the battle to rage on without me, quickly scaling the mesh cage and using it to launch myself to the overhanging awning above.

Pulling myself onto that, I leapt to the other side of the roof and, without thinking of my own safety, propelled myself into the air.

Yeah. It was pretty awesome.

When I met the ground, I let my body roll with the gravity and sprang back up, never breaking stride as I ran across the springy grass. I followed Wilcox into the building. Given how grievously wounded she was, Wilcox was surprisingly spry. She made it to the door before me and slammed it behind her, gaining a precious head start as I wasted valuable seconds breaking the heavy glass with the hilt of my sword. I reached into the hole I'd made and unlocked the door from the inside to let myself in.

Running up the Z-shaped stairs, I spared only a second to glance out the window at the mess hall. I couldn't see into the courtyard from this angle, but I was high enough to see the occasional jinni soar up into the open air above the courtyard. Deirdre, Mergen and Egya—as well as thirteen loyal jinn—were making short work of Wilcox's minions. The battle would be won—victory without casualties.

Well, victory with very few *casualties,* I thought as I made it to the seventh-floor landing.

I could hear the door to the communal bathroom fly open. Wilcox was taking refuge in a defensible room. She still had one good hand and a gun, which made her very dangerous, indeed. I had no idea what her plan was. I doubt she did, either.

She'd lost, and now she was cornered.

Cornered rats don't make plans.

But they also don't hesitate to do anything batshit crazy to get out of said corner.

I pushed open the bathroom door. Three gunshots rang out. Looking up, I saw light stream through three bullet holes about a foot above my head.

"Thank the GoneGods I'm short."

"Not 'gone' gods if you'd let me finish my ritual, you bitch!" Wilcox screamed back.

"Wilcox," I said. "It's over."

"NO, IT'S NOT OVER! They'll come back! They have to!"

"Your ritual failed. And even if it had succeeded, I doubt it would have made a difference."

Wilcox didn't respond. Instead, I could hear her mumbling to herself. I had to really concentrate to make out what she was saying ... and as soon as I was able to lock on to a couple of words, I knew her plan.

Crap.

I burst through the door and saw exactly what I'd expected. Nate on his knees, Wilcox's gun at his head. She was chanting the Incan incantation.

If she couldn't sacrifice several hundred kids to the gods, then she could still give them one.

And now that Nate was no longer under Sal's protective spell, nothing would come to possibly save him.

Nothing—except for me.

Without hesitation or second thought, I hurled my dirk at Wilcox. It whirled through the air in dazzling slow motion. She tried to veer to the right, but she wasn't fast enough. Instead of the sword splitting her down the center of her skull, it hit her just above her left eye.

Wilcox went down with a sickening thud.

* * *

Nate burst into tears—but not tears for his dead cousin. They were tears of relief, joy—tears of emancipation, of one who had finally found freedom. Sure, Nate had called me a bitch at Dr. Dewey's vigil, but in all of this, he was just as much a victim as anyone else. He muttered one word over and over again, and this time it wasn't "bitch."

"Sorry, *sorry* ... SORRY."

I thought he was looking at me, but he wasn't. He was staring behind me. I looked over my shoulder.

It was Sal. I guess, in all the chaos, the apu had found a way out of the mess-hall courtyard and came up here to see if he could help, too.

That's the thing about protectors. It's not easy for them to stop loving those they protect.

Sal walked past me, drew close to Nate and gave him a powerful hug. As he held Nate, he turned to me and said, "What now?"

I shook my head. I honestly didn't know, and at the moment I was staring at Wilcox's body. *I killed,* I thought as I pulled my sword out of her skull. *"And not a Class C Other this time. A human. Even if I argued self-defense—"*

"No one will ever know what you did here," Sal said.

This was one instant where I was glad for my little quirk of speaking my thoughts aloud.

What the apu did next was nothing short of astonishing.

He spread his hands out across the marble tiles of the bathroom floor, and right before our eyes, everything turned to rock, slowly absorbing Wilcox's body into it. Within moments she was gone, along with any trace of what I had done to her.

I made my way down the stairs and back across to the mess hall to find that the battle was, indeed, over. Wilcox's jinn had all been dispatched, and Egya's jinn were standing, frozen statues on the stone fountain. And the humans? Many were hovering near Mergen, happy to have his protective presence close by. But even more rushed to the doors as Sal and I pried their gates up high enough for a safe exit.

By the time everyone had exited the mess hall and felt the refreshing air of the fields outside, the humans spontaneously decided to hoist Egya and Deirdre into the air and crowd-surf them like rock stars. Egya was quick to get down—evidently, he did not like the attention, or the heights. But Deirdre—the changeling warrior—had finally found some acceptance here. They loved her for being a warrior. For being different. And for using that difference to save their lives.

None of them seemed to notice me, which was good. I'd lost my cherub mask somewhere in the climb over the mess hall, and the last thing I wanted was to be recognized. I was sure I'd be rewarded for saving them by being attacked. And I wasn't sure I had it in me to kill another, even in self-defense.

I might have helped save hundreds of lives—but I did so by tarnishing my own, newly human soul.

As I wandered around the field, I happened upon an item hidden in the grass. I knelt down and, to my surprise, found the mask. Touching its ceramic cheek, I imagined that I caught a glimpse of my father's own struggles in that angelic face.

Sometimes doing the right thing hurts, I thought, and then spoke aloud:

"But that doesn't make it wrong."

23

AN ENDING OF SORTS

irens climbed the hill as the students sat outside waiting for help to arrive. As best as I could tell, no one was hurt. Sure there were some scrapes and bruises, a few bloody noses and whatnot, and a hell of a lot of terrified, most likely emotionally scarred kids— but no deaths. Well, no deaths except Wilcox ... but given how Sal's magic worked, I was pretty sure her body was absorbed into the bathroom floor of the seventh landing of McConnell Hall forever.

She was gone for good. But considering what she'd tried to do, I could live with that.

Really, I could.

I didn't wait for the police to show up. I just walked behind the mess hall and into Gardner Hall's basement, where my room and bed awaited me. I figured that if the police needed to speak to me, they could come find me where I belonged. Under my covers and away from anyone or anything.

Crawling into bed, I sighed and closed my eyes. Barely a second went by before there was a knock on the door.

I ignored it.

Then another knock.

I ignored that, too.

But when a heavy fist knocked a third time, I sighed heavily, got up and opened the door.

I was expecting a cop or ten, but when I saw Justin's bloodied smile, my heart stopped beating for a couple of seconds (and believe me, I know what it feels like to not have your heart beat).

"You left," he said. There was no scorn or anger in his voice. Just matter-of-fact, like he was trying to process what had happened.

I didn't say anything.

"The cops will want to talk to you. Well, not you, but the girl with the cherub mask."

"They'll find me eventually."

Justin smirked. "I'm not so sure. I told them I was pretty sure the girl with the angel face was actually an angel who took to the sky after she saved us."

I raised my eyebrows at him. "What?"

"I mean—not many know who you are … I mean, *really, truly* are. And those of us who do—Sal, Nate and, well, me—we all said the same thing. And that's not all. Word is getting out. Dozens of students all saying you're gone. Like Superman or something."

"Super*girl*, you mean?"

"Superwhatever," he said, drawing me in close. With gentle hands, he wiped away a few loose strands of hair from my face. "Thank you. And not just from me. From everyone. You saved us."

I blushed. "I had help."

"You did … and we're thankful to them, too. But the kid who emerged from the almost politically incorrect white sheet said you were the one who figured it all out. You were the one who saved us."

"I guess," I said, looking down.

A firm and kind finger gently lifted my chin so that I was staring directly into Justin's impossibly beautiful eyes. "Thank you," he said again as he leaned down and kissed me.

I resisted at first, but feeling his warm lips on my own, I leaned into it. It was the first time I'd kissed anyone. Alive, that is. I died when I was fifteen, before I'd had any serious suitors, and now that I was alive again … well, kissing was *good*.

Eventually, we pulled away from each other, and I thought, *"Does this mean we're an item?"*

"An item?" Justin asked, laughing. "What are you—from the sixties?"

"Ahhh, actually, that expression is from the fifties," I said. Hey, if I was going to think out loud, I might as well embrace it.

"OK, then," he said, kissing me again. "We're an item."

I shook my head. "No—not yet. I need to tell you something. And I'm not quite ready. But I don't want to start this with a lie ... so ... no. Not yet."

He withdrew, narrowing his eyes. "Not yet, but ... there's hope?"

Right thing to say, I thought (and this time in my head). "Oh, there's more than hope," I said. "But I need time to ... to figure out how to be a college student first. How about while I'm figuring it out, we have a couple of dates? Real dates. Court me like I'm a Scottish gal from the eighteenth century."

He smiled, stepped back and curtsied. "As you wish."

"Actually," I said, "Scottish suitors didn't curtsy."

"Oh ... I figured that with the skirt—"

"Kilt."

"—they curtsied. No?"

"No," I said, grabbing his hand and guiding him to my door. "They bowed."

Standing outside my door, Justin bowed. "Like I said, as you wish." And with that, the boy with impossibly beautiful eyes and perfect black hair took his leave to give me time to figure out how to be ... well, how to be human.

Again.

* * *

The next days saw a flurry of activity. Over one hundred human students dropped out, more Others moved in and the university finally found a return to normalcy that—given the circumstances—wasn't very normal.

Deirdre, Mousey Girl (whose name, I discovered, was Aimee), Egya and I buried the gargoyle, whose real name was George Paul-Henri Gardien III. We found a quiet spot not too far from the neon cross and laid his stones to rest. Since Georgie was a guardian Other, Deirdre gave him a warrior's funeral as the rest of us said our farewells.

Aimee cried.

And so did I.

But Georgie got his farewell. And in this new and terrible GoneGod World that had to count for something.

* * *

Days passed, and the routine of college life started to become ... well ... routine. Classes, dates with Justin that ended with PG-13 kissing, hanging out on campus ... the university routine I figured must have taken place in between the wild party scenes from the old college comedies. I was just finding my rhythm when one day—about a month after the O^3 party—I opened my mailbox and pulled out a letter from the Other Studies Library—apparently it was open again and I was to report to work starting Monday. I guess Dr. Dewey, the Old Librarian, had put in my application before he died.

GoneGodsDamn it!

I mean ... oh, yay!

* * *

Monday morning I walked into my first day of work. A funny-looking woman who wore a bright blue blazer and red pants greeted me. She had a name tag that read *Jennifer Brovavick* and a smile that said, *Ask me anything.*

I handed her the letter.

"Katrina Darling? I heard they were going to send me a little helper. I was half expecting an elf." She chuckled at her own joke, but

182

when I didn't, her face went solemn. "Sorry. I take it this must be difficult for you."

I lifted an eyebrow.

"You did know David. Correct?"

"David?"

"Yes, the librarian who ..." She looked at the back of the room.

"Dr. Dewey," I said. "Yes, I knew him. He was the first friend I made here."

"I'm sorry for your loss."

I nodded.

Jennifer Brovavick stood perfectly still for a moment before reaching into her jacket. "I found something amongst his stuff—he left you this." She handed me an envelope with my name on it. "Take your time."

She walked away, leaving me with a letter that was quite literally from beyond the grave. With hesitant hands, I opened it. Inside was a short note:

Dear Ms. Darling,

Regarding your inquiry as to who donated the McMahon tartan. Upon investigating the matter, I discovered that a Miss Charlotte Darling donated it. Suspecting that she is a relation of yours, but unable to give you her number directly, due to university confidentiality clauses, I gave Miss Darling a ring and—

No, no, no, no!

discovered that she is, indeed, your—

"Kat ... Katrina!" I heard an old familiar voice call my name.

. . .

mother. She informed me that she will be up for a visit at her earliest convenience. I do not know if I crossed any lines by mentioning your employment at the Other Studies Library and—

"Yoo-hooo ... Kat, dear. It's me. It's—"

wanted to give you a heads-up just in case I did.
    Your friend,
    David Dewey, the "Old Librarian"

"—Mom," the voice called out.
    I groaned. *"GoneGodsDamn it."*
    And this time I *meant* to say it out loud.

* * *

Elsewhere, not too far away —

The government, it seems, screwed her, and now she's going to die.
    She did her duty, registered for the amnesty program, scrubbed her slate clean. At least, that's what she was told she was doing. But that's just the man sticking it to her again.
    She struggles against the duct tape and rope that bind her to the chair, but she's been around long enough—bound enough of her own victims—to know that she can't break free. Not without a miracle ... and those are in short supply these days.
    The largest of her three captors stands up and casually walks over to her like he has all the time in the world. And given that they're in the middle of the woods, she knows he is right.
    "Please," she says, "I'm just a secretary working at a small real-estate firm. You have the wrong person. You have the—"

" 'Just a secretary,' she says. 'The wrong person,' she says. I will tell you exactly who you are—a vampire, a killer ... and now my prey." As he speaks he adjusts his mask, then saunters over to a table that displays several instruments of torture—fishhooks, hammers, files, saws, nails and, to add insult to injury, a bag of salt. And not the fine-grade stuff. Rock salt.

She knows there's a reason for the expression "salt the wound." It came from sickos like this guy.

And her. But no—that was before.

"I ... I'm not a vampire."

"No ... *lies!*" he screams, his voice echoing off the walls of the abandoned warehouse.

"I'm not lying. I'm not a vampire. I was ... but then the gods ... they left—you know. I became human again."

He pretends he doesn't hear her, and with dramatized movements picks up three fishhooks and a hammer.

"I'm human!" she screams, panic finally rising above the surface, submerging her. She tries to break free, but there is no hope. Her bonds are too tight, a true Boy Scout's knot; the chair too stable, cold steel to the touch.

"You know," the man says, his low voice muffled beneath his mask. "When the gods left and all the Others showed up, there was a lot of confusion as to how to deal with the sudden influx of mythical creatures. There were so many problems—fear, violence, racism ... well, *Other*-ism ... the list goes on.

"No one knew what to do about most of the problems. But the one issue that seemed most manageable was the GoneGodDamn amnesty program. I suppose they thought it was the simplest solution. Stupid little people with their stupid little *solutions*. Like signing a paper will clean all the blood on your hands."

"Please ... please ..."

But she knows that her words won't elicit mercy. She is dead. More than dead, because she'll suffer long before she breathes her last. And as that thought races in her head, she spits at him, "You *bastard*. You goddamn *bastard!*"

He pauses, hooks in hand. "Don't you mean 'GoneGodDamn bastard'?" Then he leans in, the fishhooks hovering near her eyes.

Oh god, she thinks. *He means to pierce my eyelids ... he means to ...*

But the man doesn't pierce her eyelids; instead he leans back and says, "You know, I have a thought. A win-win, if you will. I will end you quickly. Well ... quicker than I had planned, at least. But only if you answer a few questions first."

She doesn't say anything. Tears and snot roll down her face.

"Charlotte. Do you know where she is?"

She blinks. "Charlotte? Who are you talking about?"

Faster than she thought a human could possibly move, he slaps her —fortunately narrowly avoiding her cheek with the pointy ends of the fishhooks. "No, no, no ... for our bargain to work, you have to be honest. You know who I am talking about. Your sire ... Charlotte McMahon! Surely you know where she is?"

So is this what he wants—Charlotte Darling?

"You mean Charlotte Darling ... she's changed her name when the gods left." Elizabeth voice trembles as she speaks.

"And ..."

"And I ... I don't know where she—"

"Too bad," he says, and he leans in once again with the fishhooks.

"But ... but ... I know where she is *going!*"

The fishhooks hover mere inches from her vision. "Where?"

"She's gone to visit her daughter. Katrina Darling. She's a university student at McGill. She's a—"

But her words are wrenched from her throat when the man removes his cherub mask and reveals the face beneath. It's twisted, deformed in such a way that means he once suffered for a very long and painful time, every scar earned thrice over.

"Katrina is still alive? Interesting, very interesting. What's the old saying? Two birds, one knife ..." His voice trails off as if he's contemplating some long-distant memory, then his attention returns to her. "Oh dear Elizabeth, first sire of Charlotte McMahon, now known as Charlotte Darling ... I apologize. My mind does wander these days. Shall we commence to the business at hand?" At the mention of the word *hand*, the fishhooks glint, so close now that she goes cross-eyed trying to keep them in sight.

He leans in. "Don't worry. This will be over soon. You could say I'm somewhat of an expert at this. Well, 'expert' may be inflating my skills a bit too much. I'm relatively inexperienced when it comes to inflicting pain as I was often the one on whom pain was inflicted. Still … I have thought about all the ways to hurt a person for a long time. A very, very long time, indeed."

The hooks glint again.

And she screams.

ALSO BY RAMY VANCE

Mortality Bites Series

Mortality Bites

Family Matters

Superhero Me!

Orphaned Follies

Dawn of a Thousand Sunsets

Three Dead Gods

Run, Kat, Run

Encantado Dreams

The Heaviest of Burdens

Looking for a great deal? Grab these book bundles...

Setting Fires with Dragons - complete series

Mortality Bound - complete series

GoneGod World - Complete series

Series Starter - Bundle

ALSO BY RAMY VANCE

Mortality Bites Series

Mortality Bites

Family Matters

Superhero Me!

Orphaned Follies

Dawn of a Thousand Sunsets

Three Dead Gods

Run, Kat, Run

Encantado Dreams

The Heaviest of Burdens

Looking for a great deal? Grab these book bundles...

Setting Fires with Dragons - complete series

Mortality Bound - complete series

GoneGod World - Complete series

Series Starter - Bundle